MISSION INSIDE EDGE

Shyam Nair is an e-learning professional and a first-time novelist, who absolutely loves the works of P.G. Wodehouse and Douglas Adams.

MISSION INSIDE EDGE

A Cricket Thriller

SHYAM NAIR

RUPA

Published by
Rupa Publications India Pvt. Ltd 2014
7/16, Ansari Road, Daryaganj
New Delhi 110002

Sales centres:
Allahabad Bengaluru Chennai
Hyderabad Jaipur Kathmandu
Kolkata Mumbai

ISBN: 978-81-291-2482-1

First impression 2014

10 9 8 7 6 5 4 3 2 1

The moral right of the author has been asserted.

Printed at Shree Maitrey Printech Pvt. Ltd., Noida

For Mom and Dad, who I love the most,
Baba and Pappai, my godparents,
Divya, the shining light of my life,
and
Krishna, Siddhi and Deetya

Contents

1

Mehboob Café

*I*t was a late summer evening in Bangalore. Far from the heart of the metropolis, in a seedy restaurant in a godforsaken part of the city, a meeting was about to take place.

There was a good reason why the meeting place was a dingy eatery by the name of Mehboob Café. One of the two people involved in the meeting was a national celebrity, a prominent member of Team India, who would not care to be seen in public with the person he was about to meet.

This prominent member of Team India sat on a rickety chair in the restaurant, twitching nervously, sweating buckets and refusing to touch the dirty cup that arrived with the tea he had ordered. He had no intention of even breathing the air around the place for any longer than was absolutely necessary. The only reason he was even there was because the son of a bitch who had called that afternoon had insisted upon this very place. 'Safe and out of the way,' he had said in a rather oily voice. The swine had overlooked mentioning 'smelly' and 'filthy'.

Presently, a taxi pulled over and a nondescript man stepped out. He was of medium height and slightly stocky build. He wore a cheap windcheater, a pair of faded jeans and sneakers that had seen better days. His hair had been slicked back with the aid of a liberal amount of oil or gel. In short, the man blended in perfectly with the crowd in that part of town.

He entered the restaurant and made a beeline to where the cricketer was sitting. 'How would I know you?' the cricketer had asked this man earlier on the phone. 'You wouldn't...but I would know you, wouldn't I? Be there at eight and use a disguise. Moustache...cheap sunglasses...just don't stick out, unless you want to be mobbed.'

The man pulled a chair and sat down. '*Ondu* tea,' he barked to a passing waiter. He took in the untouched cup on the table, the fake moustache and imitation Ray-Bans the cricketer was wearing. 'Your driver's?' he asked, indicating the shades.

'Look, you filthy son-of-a...I'm not here to make small talk, ok? Just hand me the stuff, name your price and let me get out of this rat-hole, ok?'

'Ah! Attitude! Now, if I were you, I'd be a little careful with that, sir,' said the man sitting back with a sly smile. He was obviously enjoying his victim's plight. It was not every day, he reasoned, that you have a man of this stature by the throat. So might as well enjoy it.

'Just give me the damn thing.'

The man took a sip of tea, sighed happily and then pulled out a thick envelope from his windcheater. This he flicked across the table towards the cricketer, who grabbed at it with shaking hands. Opening the envelope, he partially pulled out a photograph. His eyes widened in terror and he quickly pushed the photograph back in.

'You filthy swine!' he swore under his breath.

The man across the table was still smiling as he leant across. 'That girl was not even eighteen, was she? And you call me filthy! That's very rich.'

Rivulets of sweat streamed down his victim's forehead. 'You…you…can't prove a thing,' he stammered. 'I'll claim these are morphed.'

'Oh? That thought did cross my mind. Actually, I don't really need those snaps. I have a full-length movie starring yourself and that dainty damsel somewhere in here,' the man said, fumbling inside his windcheater. 'Here you go.' He tossed a CD across the table. 'That's one heck of a video, man. Think of the hits it would have on the internet. Which college did you pick her at, eh? You can keep this copy. Actually, I don't even care if you claim these are morphed. I'll have them put up on the internet, just before the Pakistan series. Do I even need to tell you what would happen to your team's chances, then?'

'Please don't do this to me. I'll be ruined,' he was almost pleading.

'That you will be.'

'I will buy these off you. Just name the price.'

'I don't want your money.'

'What, then? Just name it.'

The man leant closer and said something in a conspiratorial whisper.

'W-what!'

'You heard me.'

'Are you goddamn crazy!'

'Fine...do you think it might be a good idea to send these to a news channel as well?'

'No!' he almost screamed, the panic rising in his throat. 'Alright...let's talk. What am I to do?'

'Nothing for now. I'll contact you. For communication purposes, my name is Noor. You can start with arranging air tickets and hotel bookings for me so that I can shadow you around the country...business class, please...I don't travel cattle class...,' he smiled as he rose from the chair.

'And oh! I almost forgot,' he said, producing a cheap mobile handset from his windcheater. 'Here, keep this. I will call you on this number henceforth. Wait for five minutes after I'm gone. Pay for the tea...don't tip more than two rupees...walk down this street, turn left and you'll find a taxi stand around the corner. Don't take a cab straight to your hotel. Oh! And please drink your tea.'

Saying that, the man stepped out and disappeared into the crowd.

2

The Malleshwaram Mavericks

I am just an ordinary guy. That, by itself, is not remarkable in a country where about a billion people answer to that description. Equally unremarkable is the fact that I live in a Bangalore suburb and am pursuing a degree in science. By 'pursuing' I do not mean 'hot pursuit' or anything. My attitude towards lessons is that of a tourist passing through town— admiring what there is to be admired, collecting mementoes to remember the good times, losing the way on a few occasions and generally hoping to pass through without contracting anything serious. It's the kind of leisurely approach that is easy on my nerves and for some inexplicable reason has the exact opposite effect on my father's.

But, sometimes, extraordinary things happen to ordinary people and change their lives forever. This story is about a series of such events that turned my life on its head last year.

To start with, it was a glorious day. I really wish God had left it at that. But I suppose He must have been in the sort of mischievous mood that made him plant that apple tree in the Garden of Eden, put a rather innocuous looking 'Trespassers will be prosecuted' board on it and then throw in a gorgeous chick to muddle matters.

The sky was a clear blue and a few puffs of clouds hung about in a way that was perfectly acceptable for clouds to hang about. The grass covering the ground was green, as it had a right to be and, on it, were eleven boys in cricketing whites busy making complete asses of themselves. In short, nothing was quite out of the ordinary.

'Howzatt?' I shouted, with a passion that would have shaken lesser mortals to their foundations. But the umpire was made of sterner stuff. In response to my appeal, he raised his finger, but only to dig his nose.

I looked around the field. The Malleshwaram Mavericks were all there. There was Bonsai behind the wickets, Captain Naidu at first slip, Reddy at point, Das in the covers and the rest of the team placed in positions that no reputable coaching manual would ever recommend. Yes, they were all there and, so far, they had outdone one another in giving the art of fielding a bad name.

In this, at least, our captain was leading from the front. Thrice had he shied at the stumps with the batsman well short of the crease. On two occasions the ball went for overthrows and, on the third, it caught the umpire at short-leg in the crotch. Thus, we became the only team in the glorious history of the game to dismiss an umpire before dismissing a batsman.

If I had to pick one of these fielding stalwarts to describe, I would pick Reddy. This man took the cake and the entire bakery with it! Over after over, he had stood at point with an expression that was a cross between deep thought and constipation. One would think he was casting a philosophical eye on life that was passing him by. Why he chose not to cast an eye, philosophical or otherwise, on the ball that was passing him by with alarming regularity was the kind of question that caused frustrated bowlers to queue up outside the shrink's office.

I walked slowly towards the slips, where Naidu had parked himself. On normal days, our portly skipper would be jumping all over the place shooting his mouth off. But today he was quiet. Considering that he had been giving free lessons in dropping catches, I was glad he was not exactly urging the team to take up his example.

'This thing refuses to swing,' I said, achieving the unique distinction of simultaneously talking about the state of the ball as well as coming up with a silly rhyme. The ball was now a mottled brown object of indeterminate shape. Naidu studied it in much the same way he studied his textbooks—seeing everything, comprehending nothing.

'Hmmm…,' he said, with the air of a man whose intelligence seemingly permitted him to work out the dynamics of reverse swing, while simultaneously solving quantum mechanics problems. 'Look,' I said, when nothing followed the 'Hmmm…' for a full minute. 'I can't bowl to this field. I mean, we are thirty overs into the match and we still have a slip! And that too when the ball is not swinging! Why don't you move out of slip and give me some extra protection on the leg side?'

Moving out of the slips would mean occasionally having to give chase to the ball, a prospect that would not be appealing if you were the kind that had to go to shipyards to get yourself weighed. Not surprisingly, Naidu turned me down. Instead, he did a quick survey of the field and spotted Percy Gopinath enjoying a quiet stroll along the fine-leg boundary. 'Percy,' bellowed our captain in a voice designed to bring concrete walls crashing down, 'come finer.'

But the walls enclosing Percy's brain were clearly made of tougher material. The high decibel bellow emitted by our formidable skipper only made the man stop in his tracks with a quizzical look, as if wondering what the shouting was all about.

'Finer, finer,' I shouted in far less impressive a voice. To compensate for the lack of acoustic intensity, I added enough hand signals to make my intentions clear to anyone with even half the brains of a retarded baboon. But then, Percy was the sort that would make the said baboon seem like Albert Einstein. It was no wonder, therefore, that the fool continued to stand his ground.

It was at this point that Bonsai came to our rescue. Turning to Percy, he let forth a string of expletives that, in rather colourful terms, questioned Percy's origins, expressed doubts about his ancestry, and equated him with the missing link in the chain of human evolution. Amazingly, Percy flashed a 'thumbs up' and moved to exactly where we had wanted him to be and proceeded to drop a couple of catches in that position in the course of the match.

3

An Incident at Koshy's

$\mathcal{I}$t was 6 o'clock by the time we left the ground. The evening was beautiful. The sun, ever a stickler for routine, went about its business of sinking in the west without too much fuss. Flocks of birds were flying about in random directions, in a manner that was perfectly acceptable for flocks of birds to fly about at this time of the day. In a moving testimony of humanity's harmony with nature, people and vehicles were also doing the same.

Bonsai and I set off together on his bike. In the entire team, only he had had a great day. After all, it was on the strength of his rapid-fire fifty at the top of the batting order that we had managed to pull off an improbable victory. Inevitably, the man was shooting his mouth off about how he had deftly placed the fifth ball of the fifteenth over to the right of the fielder at point, hit the bowler for three successive sixes in the twenty-sixth and, when he finally did get bowled, he smartly chose to do so off a no-ball. Had I been really paying attention to his chatter, it would all have seemed like he had brilliantly executed some master plan!

It took us about fifteen minutes to get to Koshy's from the ground. By the time we reached the restaurant, the ratio of the number of words Bonsai had spoken to that I had was something like 343,102: 6, my only contribution to the conversation being six entirely-devoid-of-interest instances of 'hmmm…'. Bonsai would certainly have done better had he not been required to stop occasionally to breathe.

Coming to Koshy's was a ritual that Bonsai and I followed after every match. To tell the truth, we were superstitious about it and had lost count of the number of victories celebrated here and the losses mourned. The place had an old-world feel. Our fathers, having been chaddi-buddies themselves, still spoke nostalgically about the restaurant. So, in our own little way, Bonsai and I were doing our bit to walk in our fathers' footsteps.

It is at this point that Bonsai makes a graceful exit from this story, paving the way for a character of far greater significance. He will, of course, continue putting in the occasional guest appearance, but his time in the limelight is over.

In tribute to this departing legend, therefore, let me say a few words.

My association with Bonnagudi Sainath goes back a long way, in fact all the way back to our first day in kindergarten. We didn't really hit it off well. On the contrary, it would be quite reasonable to say that in the beginning things were rough. I distinctly remember the man trying to gouge my eye out with a Nataraj pencil at lunchtime that day.

By the time we reached the third grade, and our contemporaries had honed meanness to a whole new degree, Bonnagudi Sainath had become a laughing stock thanks to his name. We even caught teachers smirking from behind the attendance registers after calling his name out aloud during the daily mustering. It was then that I unwittingly came to his rescue by coining the moniker 'Bonsai', which was a rather clever (I thought) amalgamation of his last and first names, thereby earning his gratitude and devotion for life. The name stuck even as our then diminutive Bonsai blossomed into a full-blown tree and the same chicks that had shunned BS in the kindergarten, shattering his fifty-gram heart into a billion bits, suddenly started finding the charms of his Bonsai avatar irresistible.

So here we send Bonsai on his way, wishing from the very depths of our hearts that he continues to remain the object of the affections of the opposite sex for a long time to come, and continue with the rest of the story.

In the many months that have passed since that fateful day, I have on occasions wondered what my life would have been like had I, for once, broken with tradition and given the restaurant a miss. I think it would have been dull, boring, unexciting, mundane and, in general, very, very safe.

I heard her voice before I saw her. There were good reasons for this. For one, I had been too preoccupied to notice anything when I entered the restaurant. Secondly, the guy with her had been sitting facing her and with his back to me. Being built the way houses are, he had effectively shut her out from my view.

The first words I heard her say were certainly not romantic by any stretch of the imagination. 'If you really have to smoke, why not step outside?' The guy muttered something under his breath and walked out stiffly, as if his muscles had a tough time going about their job.

And there she was, sitting all by herself, leafing through a copy of some random magazine. Being a well-mannered sort of chap, I refrained from staring at her. Instead, I stole occasional glances at her while pretending to study the menu.

She looked very much like a lot of girls in our college, dressed in the inevitable t-shirt and jeans. But, there was something different about her. I know that sounds clichéd, but what the heck am I supposed to do? There really was something very different about her. Was she pretty? Yes, sort of. Actually, very much. When she answered her phone, she tossed her shoulder-length hair in a manner designed to keep cardiologists in business. She laughed pleasantly and ever so often there was a glint of mischief in her eyes that should really have warned me off.

The return of the ape-man caused her to say a hurried goodbye and snap the phone shut. He looked around menacingly at the few occupied tables and spotted me eyeing the girl. This made him focus entirely on looking menacingly at me. I snapped out of my reverie and, for the first time since entering the restaurant, I turned towards Bonsai, with the intention of shifting my attention to him, only to see his generous rear disappearing around the bend to the washroom.

I opened my mouth to call Bonsai back, because my in-built warning system was flashing a 'Category Red', which usually means that I'd be very soon needing reinforcements, but the words stuck somewhere in the vicinity of my epiglottis. Meanwhile, the gorilla had risen from his seat and moved his formidable hulk to a location that can be best described as 'towering over me'.

'What is your problem, you runt? You'll ogle my girl, will you?' he growled, rolling up his sleeves and flashing forearms thicker than my torso. At this point, one of the words trapped in my throat saw its chance and made a run for it. 'I...I...I...' I stammered. In one fluid movement, the guy grabbed my collar and hoisted me till my face was a mere inch from his.

'Now listen, you worthless piece of trash,' he hissed. 'If you ever ogle my girl again, I'll break your legs and stuff them down your throat. Do you get that?' I realized that my head was nodding vigourously. I was just not sure whether I was doing it on my own or if it was being done for me.

'Stop it Gaurav. Leave him alone.' The girl was standing right behind my tormentor. The guy shook me one last time and dumped me unceremoniously in a crumpled heap on the chair.

'This is the limit, Gaurav. You have embarrassed me for the very last time. Now just get lost,' she shouted and stormed out of the restaurant. The guy gave me one last, really dirty look and followed the girl out.

I did not move for about two minutes. There were very few people in the restaurant at that time, but I knew without looking that all eyes were trained on me. I was not sure if the guy would ever embarrass the girl again, but I sure had never been so embarrassed in my entire life. I was a regular here. The manager, the waiters, the chef and even some of the customers knew me. My reputation was in tatters. At that moment I wished the earth would open up and swallow me whole. But such geological events have rarely been known to occur when one needed them the most!

'Hey! You ok?'

It was Bonsai. It had to be Bonsai. Who else could be thick enough to look at a friend draped across one arm of a chair like a limp rag doll and ask if he was ok? I stared at him, uncertain what to say. 'Why was that guy roughing you up?' Another classic Bonsai question to which I had no answer.

Before I could think of one, the ever-practical Bonsai said, 'Come on, man, just forget it and let's order some food. He was a nutcase. Just have this.' I took the proffered glass of water and sipped hesitantly. I didn't even bother with the food.

Bonsai and I parted ways outside the restaurant and I walked dejectedly towards the auto stand round the corner, my head still reeling from the events of the day. I had barely turned the corner into a street when I saw the girl standing at the bus stop. I was about to dart back around the corner when she saw me. Too late! Looking around quickly to confirm that the guy was not around, I put my head down and quietly walked past her.

'Excuse me.'

My breath caught in my chest. I turned, still not able to look her in the eyes. I made up my mind to apologize for my behaviour.

'Look, I'm really sorry about what happened back there.'

Strangely, my voice sounded very feminine. It took me two seconds to realize that I was not the one speaking. Startled,

I looked up.

'I'm really sorry. Gaurav is such a jerk,' she said, reaching out to touch my arm.

I couldn't agree more. Less than an hour ago, we didn't even know the other existed and now we were already beginning to think alike! It had to be a positive sign. Suddenly, I started to feel much better.

'You don't have to apologize. It's really ok. Actually, I did look at you once or twice.'

She grinned impishly. 'But that does not give him the right to act like the complete idiot that he is in a public place.'

Exactly my point! Wow! This was just getting better and better.

'Look,' she continued, 'you must have been badly embarrassed. I really feel responsible. I'll make it up to you.' She held out her hand. 'I'm Nisha.'

'Nikhil. Friends call me Nick.'

'Ok, Nick. Friends, then?'

I was acutely aware of a little bell ringing urgently in some remote corner of my brain. I ignored it and took her hand.

Her house was on my way home. So, we decided to share an auto. For some time, an awkward silence hung about in a way that was perfectly acceptable for awkward silences to hang about.

'So, you play cricket?'

Now, let me see. I was wearing cricketing whites. A bat and a couple of pads were sticking out of the duffel bag I was carrying. Do I play cricket? No, I just love to go around town carting a bag full of cricket gear.

Needless to say, it was a very pleasant trip back home. We, or, to be more accurate, she, chatted away happily. Yet again, I was the passive party in a one-sided conversation, but this time I enjoyed it and hung on to every word.

Like me, Nisha was an only child. Her dad had retired from the army earlier in the year and taken up an assignment with a private firm in Bangalore. Her mom, like a lot of women married to army men, was a housewife. The family had come to Bangalore a week ago, which explained why Bonsai and I had never seen Nisha on any of our bird-watching expeditions. Gaurav was the son of a family friend and the only guy she had managed to befriend in her first week in town.

Unlike the heart of the poet Wordsworth, mine did not need to behold a rainbow in the sky to leap up with joy. The mere knowledge that she was sick and tired of this Gaurav character was reason enough.

We parted at the gates of her apartment, which was bang opposite the library. As I made my way home there was a spring in my step, a phone number in my pocket and a rather foolish grin on my mug.

4

A Promise Kept

$\mathcal{B}$y the time I woke up the next morning, late, even by my own tardy standards, dad had already left for work. Mom was in the kitchen, fixing my breakfast. She flashed a quick smile as I entered, yawning widely. 'Wake up, sleepyhead,' she said, tousling my hair. In many ways, mom was my best friend. I could discuss just about anything with her.

'Oh, by the way, who is Nisha?'

I was caught slightly off guard. 'A friend. Why?'

'She called a while ago. Said she'd call again.' As if on cue, the phone rang. Mom answered it and I heard her say 'Hold on, beta.' As she handed the receiver to me, I noticed the beginnings of a very mischievous grin on her face.

'Hi...nothing much...yeah, I have a round of practice at 11... After that? Nothing particular, I might hang out with the boys... No, really. Nothing fixed... Sure. I'll pick you up at five…bye.'

'Nikhil Hariharan,' my mom was sitting on the sofa, arms folded, the naughty grin having now acquired Cheshire proportions. 'Aren't you going to tell me about it?' she asked, patting a spot on the sofa.

When my mom pats a spot on the sofa, I know there is gonna be trouble. Not the you-are-in-deep-shit-Nikhil Hariharan kind of trouble but the you-better-let-me-in-on-it-or-else kind of trouble. You see, in addition to being the friendliest mom in town, she is also a big Bollywood aficionado, who had carefully modeled herself on some of the most delightfully and frightfully cool moms to have graced the silver screen. While she has donned different roles at different times, her personal favourite is that of the mom in that movie where the said character carries on comical communications with the portrait of her long-deceased husband. My mom so got into this character that I have often wondered what she would give to have dad turned into a frame on the wall, rather than have him walk around in flesh and blood.

And I could see her easing into this favourite role even as she sat smiling wickedly on the sofa. Experience has taught me that the best way to deal with the situation was to play along.

'Tell you about what?' I asked, playing along.

'About Nisha!' she said, rolling her eyes in mock exasperation.

'Mom, she's just a friend, ok?' I stressed the 'friend' a little.

'Just a friend?'

'Just a friend,' I confirmed.

She sighed deeply and dramatically. 'Well, I'm glad you at

least got yourself a "girl" friend. I was just about beginning to get worried.'

'Mom, you really must stop watching those silly movies!'

'Hey! It's half past ten. Aren't you supposed to be at the ground?'

'Good God! If I don't make it on time, Naidu will see to it that I won't have much use for a girlfriend!'

'What?'

'Er...nothing.'

I didn't do too well at practice. That, by itself, was nothing to write home about, but this time I had a real excuse. My mind was constantly wandering off towards the date I had with Nisha. I was feeling foolishly happy and was grinning at everybody, even Naidu, as Bonsai would tell me days later.

After practice and a hurried lunch with the guys, I rushed home. Even though my heart was pounding along at umpteen miles an hour, I forced myself through a bath, spent ten minutes running a razor through a three-day stubble, smuggled dad's favourite cologne from his cabinet and dabbed on a generous amount, and made several unsuccessful attempts to slick my hair into place with gel flicked from the same source. I deliberated for half an hour whether I should wear my black shirt or blue shirt and finally settled on my white shirt. I didn't have too much of a choice in jeans because only one was washed and ready to wear.

In spite of my elaborate preparations, I discovered I still had two hours to kill, time that I spent driving my usually unflappable mother up the wall. Finally, in exasperation, she threw me out of the house.

'Hey,' she said, as I was getting ready to dash out of the house, 'there's an auto strike today.'

I stopped dead in my tracks. 'Er...any chance that dad has left the car keys behind?'

'You know that can never happen, right? So you don't have much of a choice.'

I unleashed a deep, heart-felt sigh. Yes, I had no choice!

I reached her place ten minutes before time. It was another matter altogether that I had to wait a further forty minutes before she showed up. And then she flashed a smile and said a breezy 'hi', presumably in the way of an apology. I have to admit that the wait was worth it because she was looking like a zillion bucks in a short, white, sleeveless kurta and blue jeans. I was pleased to note how colour coordinated we looked.

'Well,' she said, looking doubtfully at the old Lambretta I was riding, 'Is that our transportation for the day?'

I hung my head, suddenly ashamed of the old scooter that had been in our family for three decades. It was the first vehicle that dad had ever owned. When mom and dad were dating, this very Lambretta had driven them down to Lalbagh, where the lovebirds had spent hours gazing into each other's eyes while munching on roasted peanuts. Their relationship had progressed from eating nuts to driving each other nuts and Dad had progressed from scooters to cars, but the old Lambretta hung in there.

I inherited it on my eighteenth birthday. I had actually wanted a bike. But when I saw the pride swelling in my father's chest and welling in his eyes as he handed me the keys to the scooter, I didn't have the heart to refuse.

Nisha described three-quarters of a circle around the scooter trying to figure out where to begin the ascent to the pillion rider's seat. Having apparently found one spot that held some promise, she heaved herself up and sat sideways, which happens to be the only way a girl can sit on a Lambretta unless she wants to look like she is riding a Brahma Bull in a rodeo.

Muttering a silent prayer, I kick-started the scooter and was relieved to hear the ancient engine roar to life.

We rode in silence for two minutes, aimlessly, I must add, for I was not yet privy to our destination. Finally, unable to bear the suspense any longer, I ventured, 'Are we going to M.G. Road? This road leads to M.G. Road.'

She leaned forward to answer, and I caught a whiff of her perfume. This, combined with the gentle pressure of her hand on my shoulder caused the Lambretta to wobble gently, as if it had hit an imaginary hump. 'Yes,' she said, 'in the general direction of M.G. Road.'

A vague answer such as this from, say Bonsai, would have made me want to place a well-aimed kick to his backside. I was pleased to note the utter lack of violent thoughts of any kind in response to the present instance of vagueness. It was but natural to conclude that the girl was a calming influence.

We had almost driven past the gates of the Chinnaswamy Stadium when my scooter wobbled a second time, this time a few shades more dramatically than on the previous occasion. The cause this time was the shrill 'Turn left!' she screamed in my ear that even the mandatory helmet could not keep out. 'Here?' I asked, after allowing a good ten seconds for my heart to settle, 'into the stadium?'

'Yes,' she beamed, 'I told you I'd make up for yesterday. You know the Indian team is having its nets right now and I am gonna take you inside to watch it. Live! Howzzat?'

This time my heart did leap up with joy like that of the poet Wordsworth when he beheld a rainbow in the sky. This girl would certainly keep my heart busy. Big time!

'How do we get inside?' I asked, after the initial excitement had died down a bit and my usual skeptical self was nursing thoughts of making a comeback. 'I mean, don't we need a pass or something?'

In response, she pulled out her I-Card. The word 'PRESS' jumped out at me. 'I get to go in under the pretext of covering the net session for the daily I work for.'

'That still doesn't solve my problem. How do I get in?'

Apparently, the efficient girl had thought this problem out, too. She fished out another I-Card. This she handed to me. I took a long look and handed it back to her.

'This won't do.'

'Why not?'

'My name is not Sadiq Qadri. It is Nikhil Hariharan.'

'So? You know that, I know that and perhaps a dozen others know that. No one here knows that, especially not that security guard,' she said, pointing to the robust, mustachioed specimen of a human being who, even at that moment, was walking towards us with purpose.

'Remember, you are my cameraman,' she hissed, as the said specimen reached us. I was about to point out the fact that I didn't have a beard, unlike the man whose ID it was, but by then Nisha was concentrating entirely on dealing with the guard.

We got past the guard…and it actually proved to be a piece of cake. Nisha flourished her card like they show CBI officers flourishing it in the movies. I tried a clumsy imitation and nearly poked the man's eye in the process. In the end, he just waved us through.

5

A Tryst with Destiny

It was my first time at the stadium. I had been playing cricket at the club-level for the last two years, but had never had the opportunity to set foot into the hallowed grounds of the Chinnaswamy. As I entered the stadium and saw the green turf, a thrill ran down my spine and tears of devotion sprung in my eyes. A thrill and devotion that only an ardent devotee could feel or describe. It was like the faithful had feasted their eyes upon the holy sight of Mecca. It took a lot of self-control not to fall to the knees and weep like a child. Instead, I closed my eyes and let the feeling sink in. When I opened my eyes, Nisha was watching me with a quiet smile. 'Come,' she said, taking my hand.

The practice pitches were further away. They had been cordoned off with nets and we could hear the occasional 'thwok' as wood made contact with leather. As we walked towards the nets, we saw teams of reporters, cameramen and security guards toting machine guns and stern expressions teeming around. The atmosphere seemed to be a little too charged for a run-of-the-mill net session.

And then it struck me! It had been all over the papers! Indeed, it had been all over the city and in the stadium in the form of banners and hoardings! This was to be the last practice session of the first preparatory camp for the team selected to play the upcoming five-match limited overs series against the visiting Pakistanis.

My excitement knew no bounds and I stared wide-eyed at everything. Seeing my eyes stick out like those of a frog that had seen a particularly juicy fly, Nisha muttered under her breath, 'Nick, stop staring like Alice in Wonderland. Behave like you belong here.'

Before I could come up with a suitable retort, my eyes fell upon the batsman taking guard. It was the swashbuckling opener from Delhi, the legendary Vijay Sehgal. The assembled reporters and crew greeted him with a loud cheer.

At the other end of the pitch, a vaguely familiar lanky bowler was marking his runup. I had played against the guy in a couple of local games, but just couldn't remember his name. 'Lucky bugger!' I thought, feeling a pang of jealousy. I saw two other net bowlers lined up near the bowling crease, going through a few warm-up drills. 'Lucky buggers,' I thought, feeling the pang intensify considerably. It was only the sight of Sehgal tearing their bowling to bits that eased my heart a little.

I turned to point something out to Nisha, only to find her standing a few feet away animatedly talking to someone. I literally rubbed my eyes in disbelief, because the guy was none other than Yajuvendra Singh, the dashing left-handed middle order batsman. Catching my eye, she beckoned.

'Yaj,' she said, as if she was greeting a friend from school, 'I want you to meet Nick. He is a bowler and plays at the club-level.'

The handsome bloke extended his hand. 'Howdy, mate?' he said in a passable Australian accent, presumably a legacy of his stint in the recently concluded T-20 Big Bash down under. 'So you are a player, too. Which team do you play for?'

For the next couple of minutes we spoke about cricket, he asking most of the questions and I stammering through the answers. I figured he was a reasonably nice bloke, quite contrary to the haughty, arrogant image the media had painted of him. Finally, it was his turn to bat, and he started excusing himself.

'Yaj?' Nisha asked, 'Could you do me a favour?'

'Name it, sweetheart.'

'Could you get Nick here to bowl to some of your guys in the team?'

The crazy girl had done it again! Dropped a bomb from nowhere! Her sudden request caught both Yaj and I by surprise. I adopted my classical, time-tested, mouth-wide-open-staring-into-nowhere pose, while Yaj scratched his mop of curls.

'Hmmm…lemme see. I might be able to pull something off.'

He cast a quick look at my shirt, denims and leather shoes and dished out more of the Australian accent, 'You'll have to change into more appropriate gear, mate. Wait a minute.' He hailed a ground staffer who was passing by. A quick chat ensued between the two and then the ground staffer escorted me to a room somewhere in the stadium. About five minutes later, he returned with a set of official Team India training track pants, jersey and...this is where I hold my breath until the lungs threaten to explode...a pair of brand new Nike bowling shoes!

Needless to say, I had drifted through the last few minutes in a trance. The events had left me stunned to say the least. Imagine a twenty year-old guy getting to see a legend carting bowlers all around the nets, getting to meet another legend in person and then having to deal with this unbelievable piece of generosity...all in the space of fifteen minutes! How does a guy cope with such things? The shoes were evidently a bloody expensive piece of equipment and specifically meant for Yaj... and the man had lent them to me! I was stupefied and humbled by the gesture.

Yaj and I were nearly the same size, so the clothes and shoes fit perfectly. I had never worn shoes that light!

I made my way back to the nets. Nisha quickly ran across to me, stopped just short and gave me a quick appraising glance. 'Wow! Do we look like a bowler, or what!'

'Nisha, I don't know how to thank you.'

'Shhh...Don't spoil it. Go now,' she said, sending me off towards the bowling crease in much the same way wives must have sent their husbands off to battle, when battles and such were the 'in things'.

As I stood there, with the other bowlers, I could sense my heart beating somewhere in the vicinity of my mouth. For a few moments, nobody took notice of me. Then, a dude in a safari suit and cheap sunglasses and puffed up with self-importance did and started walking towards me, gesturing and saying something illegible at the same time. Before he could get anywhere near me, Yaj boomed from across the pitch, 'He is a friend and I invited him to bowl a few overs to me. It's ok.' The safari-suited dude lost some of his self-importance and sheepishly retired to his chair.

When my turn came to bowl, I don't remember walking to the crease, picking a ball from the basket or marking my runup. What I do remember is standing at the top of my mark and looking forty-odd yards down the pitch at Yaj.

Time seems to slow down over the next few seconds. All sounds and pictures are momentarily magnified…I turn my head, as if I have all the time in the world to go about that task… Nisha is floating up and down in excitement and clapping her hands. Yaj is thumping his bat on the ground and the only sound louder is that of my heart thumping in my chest… Thud…Thud…Thud…No…the sound of my feet landing on the ground is louder… I launch myself into the air and one final thud ensues…the release is perfect…and then 'Thwack'.…

I remember seeing the famous Yaj backlift…I remember seeing the graceful motion of the bat descending to meet my half volley…I remember hearing the sound of wood on leather and seeing the graceful follow through…

What I don't remember is seeing the ball after the shot! It simply disappeared!

Strangely enough, I was not dejected that the first ball I ever bowled to an international cricketer had been so mercilessly clobbered. Perhaps, my brain was too numb with excitement to register anything. I believe that I walked back to my mark and bowled three more dollies to the champion batsman, each of which was treated with increasing and utter disdain.

As I was preparing to bowl the fourth ball, I saw a pudgy white man signaling me to stop while he laboriously made his way to where I stood. In his oversized tracksuit, he looked like someone who had never held a bat or bowled a ball in his life. In fact, he could easily have been mistaken for one of those portly, beer-drinking spectators you inevitably see on TV when the camera is focusing on their shapelier, bikini-clad female counterparts. To further lend credence to the beer-guzzler's image, this particular character had a ruddy complexion, a thick neck and an enormous belly on which a rather officious looking I-Card was currently reclining. This identified him as …someone officious…someone important enough to be able to stop emerging fast bowlers of the world in their tracks.

'Is that the fastest you can bowl, kid?' he wheezed, after waddling across the turf like a penguin with asthma.

'I can go faster, I think.'

'I think so too. It is clear that you are not putting your heart in it,' he said, tapping my chest with a thick finger. If his intention was to point out where my heart was, he was tapping the wrong half of my chest. But not being the kind to split hair over minor details, I focused on the intent rather than the scientific inaccuracy.

'Look, I want you to go full out, ok? Full out.' He spat the second 'full out' as if it were a fly that had accidentally wandered into his mouth. 'I'll be watching…from there,' he said, pointing to a group of chairs upon which a group of gentlemen was sitting. Saying so, he nodded a couple of times and waddled off in the direction he had indicated.

The effect of this incident, other than to cause a bit of commotion among the assembled armies of the fourth estate, was to snap me out of my trance. Suddenly, time reverted to its normal speed and my heightened senses returned to their normal un-heightened states.

The fourth ball, therefore, that I bowled to Yaj was delivered in this relatively calmer state of body and mind. As I ran in, I felt the rhythm syncing in perfectly. The delivery stride was good and I felt the strength surge all the way from my shoulder through my arm to my wrist. The release…was perfect.

Once more, I saw the much-admired backlift and the graceful swinging arc the bat described as it descended to meet the ball…only, this time, it met thin air.

The sound of the ball hitting the stumps was followed a second later by a collective gasp from the crowd. This was followed by a few seconds of shocked silence. Yaj looked shocked too, and was staring at the spot where the ball had pitched.

But none were more shocked than I. My follow through had taken me off the pitch to the left and I ended up close to where the fat gentleman was sitting. He nodded briefly and put up his index finger—'Can you bowl one more like that?' he seemed to ask. To indicate what he wanted me to bowl next, he held out his palm and pushed it parallel to the ground. Short ball.

This time, when I stood at the top of my run up, I dared not look at Yaj. I focused on a spot half way up the pitch instead. While I was thrilled to bits to have bowled him, I was also feeling a wee bit embarrassed for him. I could imagine what a legend like him would be feeling at having been beaten all ends up by a rookie!

The ball landed a few inches off the spot I had been eyeing and kicked off the pitch. Yaj had been winding up like a coiled spring, wanting to smash the ball to make up for the fiasco of the previous ball. Instead, he saw the ball heading straight for his melon and his eyes widened in shock. He ducked, but was a fraction too late. The ball crashed into the back of his head, and he went down in a heap.

I was the first to reach Yaj and the single thought in my head was a frantic prayer, 'Please God, let me not have killed him!' So, I was more than relieved to see him sit up, take off his helmet and rub his head. A physio raced up and held an ice pack to the spot.

'You alright, Yaj?' I asked.

He said something unprintable...along the lines of the biblical 'go forth and multiply'.

I was a bit taken aback. But then it was only natural for a batsman to react that way, especially after having taken a knock in the nut. I shrugged and walked back to the mark, glad that I had not ended up taking out one of India's top batsmen, just two weeks before the most important series in the history of two nations was about to be played. As I walked past the white bloke to my mark, I glanced at him. Without looking up from a strange device he was holding, he put up his index finger again. One more.

It made sense. Having just faced a short ball, the batsman would not be expecting another one. Just the right time to give him another nutcracker! The only thing that worried me was that Yaj would be livid by the end of it all. But somewhere deep inside I relished the challenge.

The ball landed almost exactly where the previous one had. It took off like an airplane headed for the same destination as its predecessor. This time Yaj saw it in time and swayed out of the way easily. But the effect was fairly impressive for the gathered crowd, which now also included some of the regulars of the team. They all cheered lustily, and a couple of them let out a few catcalls in good jest.

The result was that Yaj was now completely cheesed off. He yanked off his helmet and glared at me and then at his jeering teammates.

For all his bravado, however, some doubt had crept into Yaj's mind. He fished outside his off stump to the relatively full-length ball I bowled next. As I ran in to bowl the next one, I wondered if he realized that I was actually setting him up for a yorker.

Apparently he did not, because the ball swung in the air, dipped, and pitched just a little fuller than I'd have liked at the base of the leg stump, uprooting that particular piece of timber, even as Yaj's bat hung in the air, unsure if it had to descend to meet the ball.

Yaj flung his bat and walked away. I stood rooted to the spot where I had finished my follow through. The shutterbugs were busy snapping pictures, capturing videos and the reporters yapping away on their cellular phones. The buzz around the nets was deafening. In the ensuing melee, I didn't notice the white bloke until he was right beside me.

'Bill Cramer,' he said, extending a hand. I had heard the

name before, but just couldn't place it. I didn't have to struggle too much, because he solved the mystery for me. 'I am the coach of Team India. Could I have your number?'

I obliged and was asked to expect a call in a day or two.

'Yippeee!' Nisha screamed as she crashed into me out of nowhere. 'Nick, you are my hero. What an awesome display that was! You have no idea what the reporters from the other papers were saying about you,' she said, giving me a tight hug. She did it so unconsciously, that I'm sure she didn't notice the electrifying effect it had on me. This was far more thrilling than anything else that had happened that day.

6

An Extra Cozy Family Thingy

$\mathcal{I}$ couldn't wait to tell Bonsai and the rest of the gang the news. So I rushed home after dropping off Nisha at her place. When I reached home, I was greeted at the door by Bonsai. Even as I was wondering what he was doing there, he announced loudly, 'Look who's here! The hero of the day!' and, saying so, he clapped me hard on my back and gave me a hug.

Purely out of academic interest, I noted that this hug did not have the same effect as the one I had received from Nisha a while earlier and I struggled to break free. 'Get off Bonsai, what the fu...' I broke off as I saw mom rushing towards me with unbridled joy. The last time she had rushed at me like that was the day I had recited the nursery rhyme about a couple of jackasses going up some hill in search of water or something, without error for the first time. It was a different matter altogether that I had been halfway through the third grade then and the rest of the class was already reading advanced grammar. But try explaining that to a proud mother!

Pushing Bonsai unceremoniously aside, mom hugged me, making me wonder if it was one of those days! I had been hugged more number of times in the past hour than I had been in the past five years since Mishra aunty had moved out of the neighbourhood.

Seeing my dad in the living room was an even bigger surprise. 'Hi, Dad,' I ventured, wondering if he would hug me, too. Thankfully, the men of the Hariharan household are not given to such brazen displays of emotions, so he restricted himself to a nervous smile as if he was unsure of his feelings upon seeing me. I don't exactly blame him. If I had a son like me, I'd probably go around flashing nervous smiles myself.

'How come you are home so early, Dad?'

'Come, son. Sit here,' he said, patting a spot on the sofa beside him. I looked at him suspiciously. He even offered me a cookie from a plate on the coffee table, making me even more suspicious. For a fleeting second I wondered if my exam results had been declared and this extra-cozy family thingy was the proverbial calm before the storm. Were they fattening the pig before slaughter? Then I decided that there was way too much drama happening for it to be something trivial like that and put that thought out of mind. So, what was all this about?

Mom plonked herself to my right and for a few moments, I sat there, sandwiched between my parents, holding a half-eaten cookie...and still wondering what the hell this was all about!

'Hari,' said my mother, frantically flicking channels on the television, 'which channel was that, again? Ha, there it is.'

I watched as a news channel came on and an anchor began describing some sporting event in a highly hysterical pitch. The scene changed from the newsroom to a cricket ground. Then, the camera focused on a vaguely familiar figure and my mom screamed, 'There he is, there he is, there he is!' I nearly choked on the cookie when I realized why the figure was vaguely familiar. It was me!

Now everything fell into place. Why Bonsai was in my house at that odd hour, why Dad was offering me cookies and why Mom was a shade more hysterical than the anchor! I was on TV, and they were showing a ball-by-ball telecast of that spell I bowled to Yaj. I could see that the cameraman had done a great job of focusing on Yaj after each ball, capturing expressions ranging from plain outrage to utter exasperation running riot on that famous face normally used to wearing only bored, deadpan expressions even while endorsing 'revitalising' tablets.

Bonsai eventually pulled me out of the happy family tableau and clapped me once more on my back, humbly consenting to take all the credit for having discovered me as a three year-old prodigy, bowling plastic balls under-armed in the backyard.

The rest of the evening was spent answering random phone calls from people ranging between never-heard-of-relatives to my handicrafts teacher from primary school. I was elated, overwhelmed and tired all at the same time. Bonsai stayed over for dinner and looked for all money like settling in for the night and had to be finally driven out.

In all the excitement, I didn't see the five missed calls from Nisha on my cell phone.

7

Like a Fish Out of Water

*H*e woke with a start and for a few seconds was totally disoriented. The atrocious lyrics of an item number from some B-grade Bollywood flick were assailing his ears. It took him a bit to place the source of the music, and when he did, an ice-cold hand clammed down on his heart.

He picked the garish handset that was still blaring out the music, staring at it as if it was a cobra waiting to strike.

'Good evening,' the dreaded oily voice floated in through the receiver.

'Evening! You son-of-a...it is two in the bloody morning! What do you want?' he asked in what he hoped was his most-irritated voice. He would have to do what the dog asked him to, but at least he didn't have to sound cooperative.

'Ah, aggression! I like that coming from you, but only when you are on the field. If you try that tone at me again, I swear

I'll squeeze you by the balls and hang you out to dry in public. Get the drift? Don't ever forget who the boss is.'

'What do you want?'

'See, we can all be civil when we want to and that creates such a nice atmosphere to do business in.' Noor's voice had lost its threat and regained its greasy quality.

'I'm waiting.'

'I saw what happened at the nets, today. It was hilarious!' Noor sounded as if he was trying to suppress his laughter. Then he burst out in a loud guffaw.

'Yes, very funny. Now, can we, please, get to the point so that I can catch up on some sleep? I have to be up very early tomorrow.' He couldn't keep the irritation out of his voice.

'Sure, sure… let me just wipe these tears away…Oh, boy…'

For a full minute, he just heard some rustling noises. Then Noor came back on the line. 'Listen,' he said, 'I have decided to plant one more guy in the team to help you.'

'You mean one more player! You can do that?' he sounded incredulous.

'You have no idea what I can do, buster,' Noor said, sounding very smug. 'But for now you don't have to worry whether the guy is a player, part of the support staff or any other kind of waste you have floating around in the team. In fact, the funny part is that the poor bugger himself has no clue that he is being planted.'

'Then how do you plan to control him?'

'None of your bloody business, but still let me enlighten you. His girlfriend is a 'friend' of ours and when the time comes, he will do exactly as told. Men are such suckers when it comes to girls, aren't they? That reminds me, did you see the video I lent you the other day? What do you say about you and me getting into the porn business after you retire? We'll make it big, huh?'

More of the cackling laughter followed and then the line went silent.

He stood there holding the phone a while longer. Then, in disgust, he flung it away, taking care to ensure that it had a soft landing on the king-sized bed. Venting anger was one thing and losing the one source of communication with Noor was another. It wouldn't do to harm it at all, unless he wanted to have every kid and sex-starved adult in the country downloading his escapades on their systems.

It had happened the night of the last one-dayer against the touring West Indies at Nagpur. The girl had been over eighteen, he was sure of that. He had been the man-of-the-match and the girl had wanted an autograph. Like a bloody fool he had let her lead him into some sleazy hotel room…and lived to regret that ever since. The whole thing had obviously been set up.

He just could not come to terms with why he'd been picked to be the scapegoat.

8

Picked off the Streets

$\mathscr{I}$ had a restless night, having great trouble sleeping. It was close to five in the morning when I drifted away. I dreamt of many random things. In one of my dreams, Yaj was shaking me by the shoulders, screaming, 'Why? Why? Why did you do this to me? Wake up…Wake up, Nick.' I was wondering why his voice sounded so feminine. Did I hit him anywhere other than on his head? And why did he want me to wake up?

'Wake up…Wake up, Nick!'

I woke with a start, to find my mother literally shaking me by the shoulders. 'Oh! Mom, let me sleep some more, please,' I implored. This only prompted her to shake me some more. My mom can be very persistent when she sets her mind on something and, at present, she was concentrating entirely on rattling all the bones in my body.

I gave up and crawled out of bed. 'What time is it?' I

yawned. It was one in the afternoon. Mom took hold of my hand and dragged me to the living room. For a diminutive woman, my mom could display a lot of strength.

I was amazed to see Dad sitting on the sofa, eyes glued to the television set. Mr Hariharan, CEO of Hanafone, India Ltd., had taken a day off in the middle of the week! Surely, this was the end of civilisation as we knew it! I sat down, rubbing my eyes, trying to focus on the screen.

The screen was entirely filled with the large face of Mr Bill Cramer, Team India's coach. The camera highlighted the puffy bags under the eyes and the many freckles on that ancient mug. I wondered what that face most closely resembled and decided that it was a tie between a bulldog and Sir Winston Churchill.

It looked like he was addressing a press conference. When he spoke, his jowls moved as if he was chewing on a favourite bone and when he was focusing on the questions he looked grumpy, as if the bone he had been chewing on had been taken away.

While it had started registering video signals almost as soon as I sat in front of the TV, my brain took a wee bit longer to start processing the audio signals. If ever proof was needed for the fact that light was faster than sound, this was it.

'...special talent,' the man was saying, in his strange accent. 'I mean, you all saw how he made our top batsman jump around like a cat-on-a-hot-tin-roof.'

He then picked up a piece of paper from the table, pulled out a pair of reading glasses and perched them on his nose. 'Here,' he said, 'you guys are so statistically inclined in this country, so let me oblige you by reading out some stats... 81, 81,

83, 92, 94,…and hold your breath, ladies and gentlemen of the press…99…and now you can breathe again.' The gathered press reporters apparently did as they were told as was evidenced by the twitter of nervous laughter that broke out.

'Now,' he said, after some order had been restored, 'the stats I just read out are speeds in mph recorded by this speed gun when the bloke was bowling.'

A collective gasp rent the air as half the congregation gazed stupidly at the contraption the man was waving about and the other half was trying to get to grips with the significance of the numbers he had just rattled off. Someone in the crowd, apparently more the numbers-kind, asked, 'But isn't that fast? Only Shoaib Akhtar and Brett Lee have bowled at that speed!'

'Correction, my dear man,' said Cramer, 'Jeff Thomson of Australia was the first to break the 100 mph barrier. Shoaib has touched that mark and apparently so has Brett…but yes, you got my point. That is seriously fast stuff.'

'But,' began the reporter, 'how can that happen? I mean, an Indian…' he trailed off.

'I have no idea how that can happen. I just know that it has happened. Unless you are telling me that this speed gun here is defective and that the richest board in the world is doling out substandard equipment for the World Champion team to practice with.'

'Couldn't that be possible? Couldn't the gun be defective?'

Cramer sighed, pulled off his glasses, wiped them and put them away. 'Look,' he began, 'I have played my cricket in South Africa in the apartheid era and we had some seriously quick blokes. So I know fast when I see fast. To my mind, this lad is fast and he wasn't even breaking sweat. I have no idea why you folks have a tough time believing that one of you could be so good! If a Pakistani can be the fastest bowler in the world, why can't one of your lads? Are you guys any different? And just to set your mind at ease, I had one of my assistants record the speeds using another speed gun. The results are significantly similar.'

'So what's next Mr Cramer?' asked a female voice.

'Well, the contract I signed with your board included a clause that made me a selector, on par with your five zonal selectors. For as long as I am in charge of this team, I would have a say in what it looks like. So, in that capacity, I made a proposal to the board a couple of days ago. In fact, I must say I put my foot down...and it's a fairly big-sized one I got... insisting that I wanted this lad on the team to take on Pakistan in the upcoming one-day series. And, today, I got the nod from the Chairman of Selectors.'

What followed was a cacophony of noises. The visual switched to a clip showing me bowling to Yaj. I winced when this clip showed the scene where Yaj had brushed my hand off. They also showed the clip where he was dramatically flinging his bat away...three times...

Mom, Dad and I were a picture in rapt attention. Then Mom covered her face and, from the gentle shaking of her shoulders, I could make out that she was sobbing softly. I stole a glance at Dad and saw him fiddling with his glasses and pretending to be wiping some imaginary dust particle that had got into his eyes.

Like the great P.G. Wodehouse says, it is difficult to stagger when one is seated on a plush sofa. But when the thought that I was in the squad started slowly descending into my cranium, I did stagger.

The pandemonium in the conference room had been apparently restored and Cramer was set to face the barrage of questions once more.

'Mr Cramer,' began another voice, 'in this country, we don't have a tradition of picking cricketers off the street.'

'He has not been picked off the streets. He is a bonafide cricketer at the club-level.'

'But he has no experience at the first class level!'

'I don't care. He is good.'

'This is unprecedented!'

'Picking a sixteen year-old to tour Pakistan and face Wasim and Waqar at their best was unprecedented. But you guys did it.'

'Are you willing to put your neck on the line, Mr Cramer?'

'In case you didn't notice, ma'am...I have done just that. I did that when I took this job. I am doing that when I recommend that this boy be picked. I shall continue to do so till such time that you and your board are willing to put up with me. And if we have no further questions, I'd like to take your leave. You have your reports to write and sensations to create...and I have a series to win. Thanks for your time.' Saying that, he noisily pushed back his chair and moved his considerable bulk out of the screen.

I do not know if picking a sixteen year-old to play test cricket or picking a random guy 'off the streets' to play in a crucial series against your arch rivals was unprecedented. What I do know is that the flow of emotions in the Hariharan household at that moment certainly was. Mom had recovered from her sobbing fit, but stray tears did run down her face occasionally. Dad was making a heroic effort to hold back the pride he felt and the tears that were misting his eyes over. I must admit I was quite moved and was mentally cautioning myself against any remote possibility of joining forces with my parents. It simply wouldn't go with the image!

My phone rang, and I was pleased to see it was Nisha. She had been absconding lately, and I had hardly spoken to her in the five days since our trip to the stadium. 'Hi,' she burst out as soon as I picked the phone, 'before anything else, congratulations Nick! I just don't know how to say this but I'm so proud of you...so damn proud of you. Can't believe that a friend of mine has made it to the team...and will be playing for the country! Yippeeee...'

I laughed at her child-like enthusiasm. Moreover, I was genuinely pleased she had called. I had missed her over the last few days. 'Where have you been?' I asked.

'Didn't I tell you? I had this tennis tournament to cover in Mysore? Yeah...but now I'm back in town and, Mr Speedgun, you are meeting me tonight. I am not listening to excuses. Pilfer some good amount from your dad's wallet because I'm gonna fleece you. Hey, gotta rush. I'll see you at Koshy's at eight. Ok, bye.'

She breezed through the conversation before I had time to fully register that she had actually called. For several moments, I stood with the phone in my hand and a stupid smile on my face.

There were several congratulatory calls from an assortment of folks after that, but my mind kept wandering back to her call. Relatives, neighbours and friends continued to trickle in that afternoon and early evening and the house resembled a flood-relief camp with people occupying all available space and furniture. But all I could think about was our date at Koshy's that evening. I had hardly known Nisha six days! And we had barely gone out once in that time. How could I be falling for her? But somewhere deep inside, my heart knew the truth. It didn't matter…I was falling for her.

That evening, I spent a good hour decking up for the date. I raided my dad's stocks to access the essential toiletries and picked out a favourite blue shirt and a pair of fresh jeans. By the time I was done, I was a regular dandy and quite ready to paint the town red.

I walked into the restaurant a good fifteen minutes before eight and made straight for the comfortable table in the corner that I had booked.

At eight and, entirely in agreement with the formal setting, I was served a note on a plate. It was from Nisha. It read:

Dear Nick,

I'm so sorry I won't be able to make it to our date tonight. Something really urgent came up. I'll be out of town for a week or so. By then you would be in Chennai, if I'm not mistaken. I'll call you. Please accept my apologies for tonight. I'm feeling like a total dope for not turning up and not even calling you. Best of luck, champ. Make me proud.

Yours,
Nisha

9

Meeting the Men in Blue

$\mathcal{I}$ flew to Chennai for the final conditioning camp before the team headed to New Delhi to take on the Pakistanis in the opening game at the Kotla. Why Chennai, one might ask, for the conditions at the M.A. Chidambaram Stadium were entirely unlike what one was expected to encounter in the northern states at that time of the year. And our first two outings would be in New Delhi and Mohali. Chennai was the place you'd go to if getting sapped of all energy and becoming more shriveled than a raisin was your kind of thing. Yet the wise pundits who ran the game had chosen to arrange a 'conditioning' camp in this southern port city. It was like training in the Sahara in preparation for an Everest ascent.

On the way to the stadium, I thought of Nisha. It had been a week since that fiasco at Koshy's and I was yet to hear from her. I had tried calling her as soon as I received her note and many times thereafter, but her phone had been switched off. I even gathered the courage to walk up to her apartment, but found the door locked. She had simply disappeared.

I couldn't help thinking that she had simply walked into my life, worked a miracle, and walked off. What I found difficult to explain was the heaviness I felt in my heart.

To say that the week gone by had been eventful would have been the understatement of the year. It was the biggest circus of my life!

Initially, the excitement was very much there. All of us got our kicks out of answering the door to welcome fresh batches of friends, relatives, well-wishers and the like, who turned up in unprecedented numbers to congratulate me on my selection into the team.

The first couple of days, Mom would drop whatever she was doing and rush to answer the phone each time it rang; it was invariably some relative, or friend, or acquaintance at the other end wanting to talk about my 'stupendous' achievement. We were all overwhelmed and humbled by the good wishes that were being showered on me, but the initial excitement eventually wore off and finally Dad took the phone off the hook.

Every evening, the hitherto quiet Hariharan household turned into one big party scene, with not less than ten guests at any given time. The consequent unexpected expenditure was beginning to severely strain the finances, quantified by the deepening of the frown lines on Mr Hariharan's forehead.

Then, somewhere around the middle of the week, a communication arrived, contracting me to the Board for the season for a sum of ₹ 30 lakh. This alleviated the situation somewhat and caused some of the frown lines to disappear. It was a 'C Grade' contract, the lowest on offer, but I was now a professional cricketer. And all this before I had played even one day of first class cricket!

The Mavericks gave me a rousing reception. The fervour was only slightly dampened by an emotional speech delivered by Naidu, in which he conferred upon me the 'horrific' title (it certainly wasn't an 'honorific' by any stretch of the imagination) of 'The Loin of Malleswaram'. A loud cheer went up at this. Encouraged by the rare display of support, the bloody fool went on to thank me profusely for introducing him to three different virgins.

The rest of his words were drowned in a sea of catcalls and wolf-whistles...and all that the man had been trying to say was that I had introduced him to three different 'versions' of slower balls.

Overall, it was one helluva hectic time for me and my family.

Since my participation in the Bangalore camp had been limited to just bowling the ten-odd balls that I sent down to Yaj, the board deemed that I had to do more to get attuned to the rigours of international cricket. Consequently, a hurried training and fitness camp had been put together for me at the National Cricket Academy. I trained under the watchful eyes of two former greats of the Indian team, both accomplished stalwarts of their times from my state. In that one week, I learnt more than I had in the last three years at my club.

Consequently, I felt a little better prepared by the time I reached Chennai. Some of my awe of cricketing legends had worn off. Or so I thought, until I met the full contingent for the first time.

As I walked into his office, coach Cramer, or Bill as he was called, looked at me and the multiple folds of flesh that constituted his face briefly rearranged themselves into what looked like a smile. I was a tad disappointed at this lukewarm reception from the man who had, apparently, moved heaven, earth and quite a few fat asses occupying the high chairs of the selection board to get me on the team.

As I tailed Bill to the field, I could not help but think that a few days ago I was just one among the millions of fans of this bunch of Gods that I could see sweating it out in the cauldron called the Chidambaram Stadium. And today, a strange quirk of fate had thrust me in their midst.

The first one I met was Manoj Dubey, the captain. I had not had the privilege of running into him on that fateful day in Bangalore. Upon seeing me, his face burst into the famous smile that leapt out at people from TV commercials, roadside hoardings and billboards, encouraging them to buy products ranging from pens to biscuits to cars.

'You must be Nick.'

Yes, I was Nick. Even if I had been Bonnagudi Sainath or Tennamutthu or D. Nityanand, I would have confessed to being Nick or any other name he chose to confer on me. So awestruck was I that the captain of the team was even talking to me, let alone the fact that he knew my name! I later reasoned that the captain had every business knowing the names of people he was supposed to lead, but still, to me, it was a big deal.

I took the proffered hand almost reverentially and struggled not to beg him for an autograph. 'Big fan, sir,' I mumbled. The captain laughed easily, and I noticed crow's feet and worry lines on the face that appeared so flawless in the commercials. 'Monty,' he said, 'the team calls me Monty. Bill, I'll take over the introductions now. Thanks.' The coach waddled off purposefully, like a duck heading off in search of a pond on a hot summer day.

Monty led me to where three guys appeared to be standing at the vertices of a roughly equilateral triangle and gently lobbing a cricket ball between them. On closer scrutiny, it became apparent that they were practicing low catches.

'Guys, I want you to meet Nick. Nick, do these guys need an introduction?'

The answer to that question was no. The guys needed no introduction. If anyone in this cricket-obsessed country feigned ignorance about the existence of a certain Vijay Sehgal, he was either lying or being dishonest or simply not speaking the truth. After all, wasn't Sehgal easily the most destructive batsman of our times? Looking at the affable, almost goofy smile plastered on his face, one would scarce believe that he played starring roles in nightmares that bowlers the world over had nightmares about. His entire demeanour spoke of a lazy, laidback attitude. However, when he took my hand in a firm grip, I knew why balls stayed hit when he hit them.

Girish Gupta, his opening partner, on the other hand, came across as a rather shy sort of a person. Considering that I myself was coyer than a bride on her wedding day, this observation was quite rich. However, the southpaw from Delhi did give the impression of being a rather introverted person when compared to his more boisterous partner. Gupta smiled and held out a hand in welcome.

Thrilled as I was to be introduced to the two dashing opening bats from Delhi, it was the third man in the group, Roshan Saxena, whom I was really looking forward to meet. At six feet five inches tall, India's premier fast bowler towered over me by a good four inches. He'd have looked more at home on an NBA team. From that great height, he looked down at me like a hawk eyeing a mouse. His beak-like nose and deep-set eyes gave added credence to the hawk analogy. I smiled and held out my hand. Though he took it in his bucket-sized mitt, I sensed no warmth. The smile on his lips did not reach his eyes.

Before I had a chance to figure this guy out, I sensed the entire contingent gathering around me like a bunch of school kids around the ice candy man. It was a nerve-wracking experience because they were all, without exception, my heroes. The introductions were quick and brief. At the end of the exercise, I realized that my new colleagues could be bucketed into three distinct categories based on their attitude towards my inclusion in the team—For, Against and Who-Gives-a-Damn.

The knowledge of the existence of these categories and who belonged where would stand me in great stead in the following weeks.

I had my first nets with the team about half-an-hour after stepping onto the turf at the Chidambaram Stadium. In that time, I had barely managed to change and do a quick warm-up. In spite of all the excitement, I noticed that Yaj had stayed away from the introductions, choosing to bat on against a bowling machine instead. Uncertain how he would react, I decided to give him a wide berth for the moment.

The team had youth and experience in good measure. The experience came in the form of Monty, Yaj, Girish, Vijay and Gurmeet 'guru' Singh, the legendary offie, just to name a few. The youth brigade was led by Viraj Kapoor and Sumesh Rana, both middle-order bats, Raj Samra, the young dasher from Mumbai, and Roshan, Shiv and Pavan, the quicks, again just to name a few. And I, of course, was the baby of the team.

The next few days were extremely busy. Being the rookie, I was put through the grind by both captain and coach. Thanks to the big hype that had been generated around me by the media, every batsman in the team wanted to face me in the nets. Consequently, I ended up bowling the longest spells. Sensing a potential burnout in the offing, Bill asked me to go easy and not really exert myself. Consequently, I bowled at a leisurely pace and the batsmen usually had a field day. This forced regulation of pace, I realized, gave me better control of the ball. Instead of relying on raw pace alone, I was discovering the benefits of swinging the cherry and getting it to seam off the wicket. While I'd continue to bowl in the high eighties and nineties, I'd use faster balls as surprise weapons only.

Watching the other quicks in the team, I picked up a couple of slower deliveries as well. One involved cutting my fingers across the seam. The other was slightly trickier, involving releasing the ball from the back of the hand. The key to both deliveries was to not slow down the arm speed and to land the ball at a good length.

Although I was a long way from being a complete bowler, I realized that I was definitely on my way to becoming a better one.

Fielding was another aspect of the game that I really enjoyed, apart from bowling. Back home, when I played for the Mavericks, I used to field in the circle in close-catching positions. However, in Team India, I realized that most of my fielding would be as a boundary rider. This, again, was a consequence of being the youngest bloke in the team. The established royals only reluctantly ever agreed to step into the outfield.

After a couple of days I grew comfortable in my new fielding role and actually began to enjoy the sliding stops, relay throws and anticipation that was required to do well at the boundary. My strong throwing arm was an added advantage.

Like every batsman dreams of turning his arm over just for a couple of overs at least, every bowler also dreams of winning games with the bat. I was no exception. For the club, I would often come in at number seven, just after the specialist batsmen and the wicketkeeper and give a fair account of myself. Although I was no Bradman, I was no mug with the bat either. I loved to give the ball a fair bit of a tonk and had, more often than not, chipped in with reasonable contributions with the willow.

This aspect of my game showed the greatest relative improvement under Bill's watchful eye. For the first time, I began to appreciate the fact that batting was not always about throwing the kitchen sink at the ball in the optimistic hope of carting it to the cow-corner. I learnt to appreciate the finer nuances of the art, including the merits of a tight defense and a sound knowledge of where one's off stump was.

We partied hard the final night of the camp, prior to our

departure for New Delhi. It had been ten tough days at the conditioning camp and we were all thrilled about the break. I was all set for the biggest adventure of my life.

I pondered over the last few days of my life. For the first time, I had a brief insight into what it meant to be a cricket star in India. I had seen fans waiting hours in the scorching Chennai sun and then clambering over one another just to get a glimpse of their cricketing gods, as our bus pulled into the stadium each day. I began to appreciate the fact that autograph-seekers, the flashing cameras, the security cover, the myriad reports in the newspapers and on TV, the comments of armchair critics and a million other things that the common fan could not even begin to imagine were a part and parcel of a cricketer's everyday existence.

Does someone get picked from complete obscurity and thrust into the limelight overnight? Is this even fair? What about the thousands of talented cricketers across the country who while away entire lifetimes playing domestic cricket, hanging on to the flimsy hope of getting that coveted call from the selectors? Why was I the chosen one out of those thousands? Do I even belong here? Could this have happened had I not met Nisha?

Thinking of Nisha made me remember that I hadn't heard from her in a long time. With a heavy heart, I gazed out at the sea, even as my colleagues partied away into the wee hours of the morning.

10

Inspector Chinnappa

The man squatted on the floor of a dingy cell in the police headquarters, shivering despite the stifling heat. A constable entered the room and shoved a glass of water into his hands, which he gratefully gulped down. He hadn't had a sip since the previous evening, after he had been picked up by the cops from Moonlight Bar.

He had just been at the wrong place at the wrong time. All he had wanted was to have a good time with his girl in one of those tiny rooms they had at the Moonlight. The cops had come out of the blue and dragged him out in his underwear. They had been a little more considerate with the girl, letting her throw on some clothing before escorting her out as well.

The door of the cell opened again and an inspector walked in. He could tell the difference between an inspector and a constable, since he often ran into members of the force in his line of business.

The inspector pulled up a chair and sat down.

'Amit Singh?'

The man nodded.

'You have had a lot to say since you got here, so my men inform me.'

'I've...I've heard a few things,' he stammered.

'Like what?'

A hint of defiance crept into his voice. 'I already told the cops who picked me up yesterday.'

The inspector picked up a device lying on a table and switched it on. 'I'd like to record your statement. Do you mind saying it all over again?'

'Recorded statements cannot be produced as evidence in court.' The defiance had gone up a notch.

The inspector rose from the chair, calmly replaced the device on the table, walked over to the man and slapped him tight across the face.

'Now, can we go on?'

He nodded weakly from where he had fallen on the floor. He was in no mood to endure any more of the interrogation methods the cops had employed on him the previous night. Mentally, he cursed the moment he had let out the secret in a drunken stupour.

'We can start whenever you are ready or in the next five seconds...whichever is earlier.'

The man sat up slowly, his face still stinging from the slap.

'I heard it from my girl...I can't be sure about it.'

'Go on.'

'My girl works at Moonlight Bar. She...she heard from... from one of her customers.'

'M-hmmm.'

'The guy was called Noor.'

The inspector turned to a constable standing nearby. 'Interrogate the girl. I want a detailed description of this Noor. Get a sketch prepared at once.'

'This Noor came to the bar three nights ago. That night he was high on booze and hash and...and said something to my girl, who was with him.'

The inspector waited patiently for the wretched man to go on.

'He said that he was going to earn a lot of money very soon and that he'd take her to Dubai on a honeymoon. He said he had worked out a deal with some player in Team India that was gonna earn him millions. He was bragging about how he had this guy by the balls and how he could make him dance to his tunes.'

'Did he give a name?'

'No.'

The inspector put the device back on the table and prepared to rise from the chair again.

'No...No...he really didn't give out a name...I swear to God.'

'You better be clean about this, because if I find out you were lying...'

'I swear to God...he didn't give a name.'

'Has this...Noor...come back to visit your girl anytime after that night?'

'No.'

'Do you know where he might be found?'

'No.'

The inspector turned to the constable. 'Take him and lock him up. What charges have been pressed?'

'Illegal gambling, illicit liquor.'

'Cook up something more…make it non-bailable…I want him in for as long as it takes to investigate this case. Make sure the girl gives a detailed description for a sketch. I will see her after that.'

The inspector walked out of the cell to a room where a senior officer had been listening in on the conversation.

'What do you make of the case, sir?'

'I think he has told us all he knows.' The senior officer scratched his head and sat behind his desk. 'Look, with the type of guys that frequent Moonlight Bar, I wouldn't rule out the involvement of a betting ring. That logically leads to a possibility of match fixing, as we have long suspected.'

'I think so too. I just want him and the girl to be locked up safe so they have no chance of alerting this Noor person.'

'That's a good idea. So, what are your next steps?'

'Preparing to tail the team as planned, sir, with your permission. Need to zero in on this rat in the team, before he sinks the ship.'

11

On a War Footing

$\mathcal{O}$ur plane touched down at New Delhi's Indira Gandhi International Airport on the morning of 12 April. The first word that crossed my mind upon seeing that magnificent aerodrome was 'Big'. My previous encounter with airports having been limited to the ones at Bangalore and Chennai. I wasn't exactly an authority on airport sizes, but this had to be one big momma of an airport. The sights and sounds of the place ensured that the *Alice in Wonderland* expression was beginning to take up permanent residence on my mug.

For the massive hotel rooms, again, we were thankful, because two of us had to share one. Indian teams of the past had done away with the roomie-system, assigning individual rooms to even the junior members of the squad. However, Bill would hear none of it and actively promoted the reinstating of this practice, insisting that it would help build camaraderie and team spirit.

Ironically, it almost had the opposite effect to start with. The seniors, who were used to being treated as royalty, desperately tried to move the coach from his stubborn stand, but eventually gave up, sensing that moving the Rock of Gibraltar would have been an easier proposition.

Giving further proof to the notion that we were dealing with an oddball of a coach, Bill figured it would be a great idea to pit people from the extremes of the spectrum together. To him it made perfect sense to have a batsman room with a bowler, the logic behind this line of thinking being that the roomies would give each other an insight into the two different trades they plied.

I'm not sure if this worked for everyone, but it surely worked for me. I was to roost with the very companionable Vijay Sehgal. I hoped to spend a good part of the next two weeks picking his brains and coming away with enough tips to appreciate the mindset of a batsman. I also hoped against hope that the words of wisdom from this legend of the game would help me take rapid strides as a batsman as well.

The practice facilities at Kotla were very good. You had to hand it to the Board. They did a fantastic job, pampering us with great training facilities, well-equipped gyms and excellent nets. The security was very much there and very 'in-your-face'. But that was to be expected for a series of this importance. Political big-wigs belonging to parties of all hues from either side of the border were expected to attend the games. The gun-toting members of the constabulary were, therefore, a constant presence.

Having bowled all my life with the red duke ball, I was only just coming to terms with the white kookaburra, which, for reasons unknown, was the preferred ball in the series. Perhaps the tournament sponsors or the ICC had something to do with it. So, the coach and his assistants devoted extra time towards getting me to literally come to grips with this ball.

It was while reflecting upon the difference between these two makes of cricket balls that some immortal words uttered by the legendary Kaju Kesarvani during one particularly animated drinking session came to mind. Having downed three whole Kingfishers and made steady progress on the fourth, the man had declared that the world was made up of two kinds of things—things that swing and things that do not.

'For instance,' he had slurred into the ears of his immediate neighbour at the table, 'let us take Suchitra N's bum...'

'Must we?' slurred this particular neighbour in return, trying hard to focus on Kaju's hands, which were held out in a manner reminiscent of holding the aforementioned derriere.

'Oh, absolutely. It swings...like a pendulum...tic...toc... tic...toc. However...' and here Kaju paused for effect, 'her sister Sujata N's bum. Now that is a different case altogether...It...'

Kaju didn't get any further on this lesson on aerodynamics, because the neighbour at the receiving end of this Kingfisher-powered discourse happened to be none other than Sukesh N, the lone male sibling of the two subjects of Kaju's simple harmonic observations.

This lone male sibling then proceeded to pound the hapless and entirely clueless Kaju to within an inch of his life.

What became of this Kaju? Did he continue pursuing his

scientific endeavours with zealous fervour even in the face of violent repercussions at the hands of male relatives of his female subjects? Did his unusual first name have anything to do with the unusual shape of his head? These, and other such questions, are of mere academic interest. Even as the legend of Kaju was consigned to the pages of history, his immortal words lived on and came unbidden to the mind as I pondered the difference between the duke and kookaburra ball. The former swung and the latter did not. Well, at least not as much.

I noticed that the duke had a more pronounced seam and therefore was better suited to seaming and swinging conditions, such as in England. The kookaburra seam, on the other hand, was not as prominent. Theoretically, it should not have swung or seamed as much as the duke.

Here is where I found an anomaly. At a certain speed and with a particular combination of atmospheric conditions, the kookaburra did swing appreciably in the air. The set of parameters required to get the ball to 'do things' in the air and off the pitch were very particular and it took a lot of practice and patience to get the pieces to fall into place. I guess the swinging abilities of this brand of ball were also due to the extra lacquer applied by the makers to maintain the shine longer.

By the time the day of our arrival at New Delhi had drawn to a close, I had become more confident in my ability. The ball was beginning to respond to my commands and I had added and honed enough deliveries into my repertoire so as not to become predictable. Even as the first match approached, I was ready for action.

Like men of the armed forces, we cricketers were also not

supposed to divulge details to even members of the family. Not that my mom would be interested in pitch conditions or weather reports or team compositions, but it was a matter of protocol not to leak out information that may be detrimental to the success and integrity of the team. These words I have picked straight from an email Bill sent to the team.

I called up Bonsai and asked him to check on Nisha. Although Nisha had, for all practical purposes, ceased to be part of my life for about a month now, I still could not stop sighing like a rice cooker releasing pent up pressure each time I thought about her.

12

The Battle of Kotla

*T*he first match, being a day-night affair like all the matches in the series, was scheduled to begin at 3:30 p.m. local time. We had an early net that day and I was pleased to see that my rhythm was good and I was working up some neat pace. So, when Bill pulled me over, I presumed he wanted me to get off the nets and start preparing for the game. I could not have been more mistaken.

'Nick,' he said, putting an arm around my shoulder, 'I want you to sit this match out.'

The words were like a kick to the guts and I was shaken to the core. 'Why, Bill?' I managed to squeak out.

'This is Kotla, son,' he replied, patiently. 'This pitch is for the spinners and Monty wants to play two spinners, so Guru and Ash get the nod. Roshan and Shiv are automatic picks, so we don't have room for you, buddy. Hard luck! But you are the twelfth man for the game.'

I didn't know whether to be distraught at not making my first-class debut or happy in the knowledge that I was at least the twelfth best player in the squad. But there was really nothing I could do. While the selected eleven went into final preparation mode, I resigned myself to setting up bottles of water and energy drinks and to sulking on the sidelines.

All my life I had heard commentators attempt to describe what a full stadium sounded like. I now knew first hand. Deafening, pandemonious, cacophonical…in other words, pure, unadulterated noise. Fans from both sides came in as early as two in the afternoon for a match that was to begin at half past three. With them came drums, cymbals, bugles and horns…in short, anything guaranteed to make a lot of noise. The notorious vuvuzelas made a grand comeback and enjoyed their hour of glory before being confiscated and banned again.

The game began with Monty winning the toss and inserting the opposition in, giving our spearheads another chance to exploit the early life in the pitch. As our team took to the field, I settled into a comfortable chair on the balcony, with Bill, the support staff and the four other boys who had not made the cut.

'Here we go, my boy,' said Bill, handing me a mug of coffee, before laboriously lowering his considerable bulk into the chair beside mine.

'I thought we were planning to bat first, Bill.'

'The dew factor, son. Monty spoke to the curator before the game. He thinks that in the evening the dew would settle in. Do you have any idea how it feels to bowl when the outfield is soaking wet? The ball feels like a bar of soap. Guru and Ash would hate that.'

He broke off as the Pakistani openers walked in to the middle to a mixture of cheers and boos. The much-awaited series between the cricketing world's archest rivals was just minutes away from a kick off.

'Nick, that boy Javed Salim, who is taking guard now is an unknown entity. He...what are you smiling at?'

'No...nothing...just that the name is a bit odd...here, in Bollywood...you know, the Hindi movie industry, we have a writer duo called Salim-Javed...'

'Do they write funny stuff?'

'Er...no. I think they write pretty serious stuff. Why do you ask?'

'You were smiling...so I wondered...'

'Well, I just found that name a bit odd...that's all...Sorry, Bill, you were saying something about this Jave...'

The words froze in my throat as I saw the first ball of the series disappear into the crowd. Roshan had bowled short and wide outside the off stump, an offering that no batsman since the time of W.G. Grace would have missed.

'Mother of God,' mumbled Bill, half admiring the shot. His teeth were on display to those members of the paying public that were staring at the giant screen, for some camera had chosen to capture the grimace on his face at that precise moment.

Five overs into the game, we had our heads in our hands, hardly able to believe what was happening out there in the middle.

What had followed that atrocious first ball was an even more bizarre display of senseless bowling by both new ball bowlers. They continued bowling short and wide and on the occasions when they tried to pitch it up, they ended up spraying the ball all over the place.

The Pakistani openers had a field day! Not once did they look in any danger of getting out. By the fifth over, they had amassed fifty runs, and I had amassed a massive headache. I glanced over at Bill. His face gave nothing away, but his eyes were taking in the carnage that his wards were suffering at the hands of the marauding Pakistanis. The Kotla crowd had gone dead silent.

'Nick?' asked Bill, cradling his coffee mug in his palms, 'what do you think we must do?'

'Huh?'

'What should we do now? How do you think we can stem the flow of runs?'

'You...you're asking me, coach?'

'You are the only Nick around, aren't you?'

Yes, I was the only Nick around. I was also the only 'very surprised' Nick around. Not to mention the only 'completely taken aback' Nick around. Me, the rank rookie of the team, tell him, the coach of Team India, what to do in a situation like this! That would be like giving Genghis Khan advice on a war strategy. Preposterous!

I looked intently at that ancient mug for telltale signs that the man was joking. The multiple folds did not as much quiver, as those intelligent blue eyes gazed right back at me.

'Well,' I began, 'I think we must not take the bowling

powerplay after the ten overs. We must take Roshan or Shiv, or both, off the attack and bring on Guru and Ash. Hopefully, the Pakistanis would not be prepared to take them on so early in the game.'

The folds on Bill's face started spreading away from one another like tectonic plates during the continental drift. He was smiling.

'I want you to run over to the boundary and give Viraj this message. Ask him to pass it to Monty at the change of the next over.'

As I rose to embark on my mission, Bill caught my hand. 'Good work, son.'

As per the revised plan, Monty pressed the spinners into action earlier than he would have liked. But the poor effort with the new ball had ensured that both batsmen had their eye in and they safely negotiated the spinners. In fact, they were even openly aggressive. By the time the first fifteen overs were out of the way, the Pakistanis were sitting pretty on 123 runs for no loss. Both openers had reached their fifties and looked well on their way to individual three-figure scores.

Monty usually liked to give his bowlers a long run. But this time he was forced to change tactics and shuffle his bowlers around like a card sharp. Thanks mainly to some imaginative bowling changes and some individual brilliance in the field, we managed to slowly put the brakes on the scoring. Still, the initial momentum gathered was strong enough to take the score past the three hundred mark.

The Pakistanis had set us a daunting target of 312 runs to win under floodlights and on a pitch that was beginning to show some wear and tear.

I crowded in with the rest of the gang during the break between the innings. Monty gathered the troops for a quick appraisal of the situation. It was grim, as was reflected upon the faces in the huddle. The captain made a speech, like they show generals make to soldiers in Hollywood movies just before sending them to their deaths. Phrases like 'self respect', 'dignity', 'kick-some-ass' and 'owe-it-to-the-nation' were liberally distributed in this discourse and by the end of it, the team had worked itself up to some kind of frenzy. The course of action decided upon was for Giri to hold up one end, allowing Vijay to hit like there was no tomorrow. The rest to follow were to build on the platform set up by our openers.

When you have a mountain to climb, the last thing you want is an inauspicious start. That is precisely what we got when Vijay chipped his favourite bat while shadow batting just after this inspirational speech and just before going out to open the innings. There cannot be a worse omen for a batsman, especially for one as superstitious as Vijay. So, it was not surprising to see our champion walk out as if he was on his way to his own funeral.

Experts who have analysed Vijay's batting over the years have all commented on the great shock value it has. It shocks either the opposition or his own team.

In what can only be described as a masterstroke, the Pakistani skipper started with an offspinner. It was a move designed entirely to entice Vijay to go over the top early on. Vijay took the bait as early as the third ball of the first over. In a rush of blood, he charged the bowler and missed the line all together as he took an almighty heave at the ball. He was stumped by the proverbial mile.

In the stunned silence that followed, I looked at Bill out of the corner of my eye. The man seemed to have aged a couple of decades since the match had begun.

Some semblance of order was restored with a series of partnerships down the line. First, Giri and Viraj got together a fifty-run association for the second wicket. With Giri's departure, thanks to a piece of brilliance in the field, Yaj came in to join Viraj. They struggled over the next fifteen overs to string together another fifty partnership. With the run rate climbing with each over, inevitably some risk would need to be taken.

The intended charge never came. Yaj was struggling with the bat and barely hanging on. Viraj was clearly looking for some inspiration from his senior partner. When none was forthcoming, he pottered along, looking as lost as a kid in a strip club.

When the dust settled, we had folded up for 236, with Yaj scoring a patchy 76. The writing was on the wall.

To me, it was evident that we had not used the new ball well. Both Roshan and Shiv had bowled way too short, when they should have been floating the ball up to the batsman. The overcast conditions would have ensured some swing, which they could have exploited earlier on. The short-pitched stuff they dished out had certainly made it difficult for the batsmen to play too many shots, but had done nothing to force them out of their defensive mode. I just had to talk to someone to see if they shared my view.

My chance came a little later, when Vijay invited me out for a drink. I was a little wary of broaching the subject for two reasons—for one, Vijay himself had had a bad day at the office. For another, I was not sure if he would simply dismiss me as an upstart who had no business meddling in matters that were beyond my comprehension.

At that point, a third nagging reason entered my mind. If I criticised the bowling tactics of our seamers, would Vijay think I had vested interest? I couldn't think of a better way to send my fledgling career on its way to an early death.

Thankfully, Vijay provided the opening I was looking for. 'We screwed up big time, didn't we? They had us by the balls throughout.'

'Yeah,' I began, latching on to this window of opportunity. 'I was wondering if we didn't kind of hand them our balls on a platter. Should we have bowled differently with the new ball?' I gazed closely at his face to see how he was taking it and was glad to see no discernible change in expression.

'How do you mean?'

'Should we have attacked a little more? Perhaps pitched the ball up a yard or two and forced the batsmen into the drive?'

Vijay seemed to be giving my suggestion a think over. His brow furrowed and his facial muscles underwent a few contortions, telltale signs that the gears in the brain were in motion. This was in sharp contrast to the calm expression on his face while batting. Legend had it that the man did his thinking, if any, after he had smoked the ball to some far-flung corner of the ground.

'Perhaps,' he said, at length. 'In retrospect, we could have done a lot of things. We could have opened the bowling with a spinner, Ash, for example. He did so well and might have found the hardness and bounce of the new ball to his liking.'

'My point...'

'I see your point, speedy. We could have done a lot of things differently. But my point is that we didn't and it is quite upsetting. But we can't brood over spilt milk, can we?'

'Cry.'

'What?'

'The correct expression is cry over spilt milk. Not brood.'

'Who spilled milk?'

'No...I mean the expression you just used...It is not...'

Vijay looked at me as if I had lost my mind or something. He put a reassuring hand around my shoulder and said, 'Now you give it a rest and let's catch a movie or something. What's coming on HBO?'

I marveled at the way Vijay had sidestepped the issue. I was glad that he had not suspected any malicious intent in my thoughts, for there were none. But I was also disappointed that he had brushed it off so lightly. I opened my mouth to protest, but the man had clearly pushed me out of his mind and was busy draining his beer. I thought it prudent not to pursue the matter any further.

13

Foot in Mouth Syndrome

The team met in Bill's room the next day to conduct a post mortem of the performance, or the lack thereof, the day before. The atmosphere in the room would have made a funeral parlour look like the Mad Hatter's party. A number of tired and broken spirits lay strewn around in various states of depression. A very agitated captain was pacing around with a can of soft drink gripped tightly in his hand, while the rest of us waited with bated breath for him to work off some of his agitation.

The pacing around continued for two more minutes. Then, as if realizing the futility of pacing further, he stopped and turned to face us. In a rare display of thinking together as a team, the words 'here we go!' flashed through the heads of everybody present at that precise moment.

There are many pleasant ways of beginning a speech. I am not saying that Monty needed to address us as 'gentlemen' or anything, though that would have been very nice. A simple 'Hi' or something civil like that would have sufficed and done his dear grandma proud. But the word 'pathetic' seemed to express his mood better. 'Pathetic!' growled Monty. 'Disgusting,' he added for the benefit of those who had yet to come to grips with 'pathetic.' 'Preposterous,' he said in a tone that would have made the meaning of the word clear even to a passing Martian. 'Lack of heart, that's what is inexplicable. We can all have bad days at work, we can all make mistakes. Collective mistakes, even. But the lack of heart is what hurts the most.'

He paced around a little more and stopped right in front of Roshan and Shiv. 'We had a plan, Roshan. We had a plan that we had discussed inside out. Can you give me one reason why we didn't stick to it?'

Roshan and Shiv shuffled around nervously like a pair of unsynchronized dancers in a badly choreographed Bollywood number. Before they could answer, Monty continued, 'We even had a precedent from our previous wins over this very opposition. We all saw how well the tactics of pitching the ball up worked. Why, then, did we bowl short?'

'They don't play the short stuff well, Monty...and the pitch was so fresh. We just couldn't resist it.'

At that point, Monty did something that I'm sure he, when he finally calmed down, wished he hadn't. Pointing to me, he said, 'That kid over there knows how to bowl on these pitches a lot better than you...and he hasn't played a first-class game yet. He had the balls to point out the error of our ways after the game yesterday.'

Upon so unexpectedly hearing my name, I started violently,

dropping the Styrofoam cup of soft drink I was holding. This caused a stain, roughly the shape of Australia to appear around my crotch. Cursing under my breath, I grabbed at the stain, but if I thought this would make the stain disappear or turn into a more fashionable shape, I was sadly mistaken.

Even as I performed my calisthenics, which were an unappealing mixture of Shakira's shimmy and MJ's pelvic thrusts, I could feel a dozen pair of eyes boring into me. As a kid, I had dreamt of one day being the cynosure of all eyes, but this was certainly not the way I had pictured it. I knew right then that Roshan and I would never see eye-to-eye again for as long as we lived.

I shot a glare at Vijay, who was busy staring at the ceiling. The man had obviously told Monty about our little conversation over beer the previous evening.

Bill looked at me and asked, 'You think we screwed up the game yesterday?'

I didn't quite know how to answer. Then I decided that a straightforward question deserved a straightforward answer.

'Yes, I think we made a few mistakes.'

'Like what?'

Once again, I shivered through an unwanted cynosure-of-all-eyes moment and felt my legs turning to jelly. However, I also knew that I had committed myself entirely on the front foot with my previous answer and there was no turning back. So, I braced myself and answered, 'I think we should have attacked more with the new ball.'

The silence in the room, as my teammates awaited my answer had been deafening. This was now replaced with a buzz that was assuming deafening proportions.

'What would you have done?'

I turned to Monty who had asked the question. Before answering, I studied his expression briefly. I could detect nothing but curiosity in his eyes.

'Monty, with all due respect, I would have pitched the ball up a little more, than try to bang it in…would've given it more of a chance to swing. By pitching short, I think we failed to make best use of the conditions. We allowed the batsmen to settle.'

'Did you even for a moment consider the possibility that bowling short was actually part of a strategy? Did you, Mr Smartass, fail to see how scuffed-up the ball was by the time Guru and Ash took over? And who doesn't know that the kookaburra does not swing as much as the duke? So what is the point pitching it up?' This time it was Roshan lining me up for some treatment.

'Roshan,' I began, 'the kookaburra does swing. I have swung it in the nets and I know that the weather conditions were just right. I just felt we didn't try hard enough.'

'Do we have to listen to just about any asshole who walks into the team?' Yaj's booming voice echoed across the room. I was stunned. We hadn't exactly seen eye-to-eye ever since I had joined the team in Chennai, but I hadn't expected this. I had no idea how to react to this outburst and decided to remain silent. Anyway, I wasn't sure if I was meant to answer since the man had just aired his views in an open forum, albeit rudely.

'Yaj, you'll take those words right back. Nick was just answering a question we asked him and I think he has a point.

We certainly screwed up big time yesterday. We simply cannot afford to make elementary mistakes like that and still hope to win the series.'

Silently, I applauded the courage of my skipper in standing up for a novice against his senior-most batsman. Vijay and Guru also threw their lots behind me and chastised Yaj. While their support was heartening, it upset me to see bad weather brewing within the ranks and that I was unwittingly in the very eye of this storm.

Over the next hour, Monty systematically dissected the team's performance, sparing none, including himself. Along with Bill, he made us sit through endless minutes of footage, analyzing errors, seeking to identify and root out the problems.

14

Noor Strikes Again

*H*e lay quietly on his bed, while his teammates raised more hell than a pack of Huns outside. He had hung around with them a while and then quietly slipped away. Most of his mates were too drunk to notice.

The phone call would come, of that he was certain. Sure enough, the instrument buzzed. Not wanting to give the impression that he had been waiting for the call, he let the garish ringtone run its course, taking the call only at the very last second.

'Congratulations! Our business association is doing very well. Do you have any idea how much we made on your first game?'

He couldn't believe the amount he heard. Could it be possible for one slimy bookie to make so much money on a single game?

'Let's now get down to business. Remember I told you about the guy we are planting into the team? I want you to have a quiet little chat with him. Go easy on him...he's just a boy...don't break him, yet. We can leave that for later, when the bugger has outlived his usefulness.'

A shockwave ran through him when Noor told him the name of the guy he was to get in touch with. That boy!

'Noor, do I really have to be friends with that boy? I am not the best of icebreakers...and you know what's been happening...'

'Don't worry, my man...I told you I have his girl in my control. He will forget everything the moment he sees his girl. Oh, by the way, I have made arrangements to get her here too, so he'll know not to act smart. I'll send you the bill for her travel and hotel expenses.' Once more that hideous laughter gushed out of the phone and he held the instrument away in disgust.

'Listen, Noor, you have made your money. Let's call this off. I can't take this shit...this tension any more. And now you are involving that stripling? He will just goof up and blow this entire thing off. Listen to me, man...Let's just close the deal.'

'Feel free to walk away from the deal anytime, champ...but rest assured that you are neck deep in shit, buddy. If you don't want to be the country's porn sensation overnight, just play along. Leave all the planning to me. Now go get some sleep... or is that not possible unless you've had some...fresh meat, eh?'

He snapped the phone shut and downed two cans of beer in two long draughts. Then he flung himself on his bed, burying his head in the pillow. He couldn't believe the disgusting things he was doing. He still felt filthy about the girl, but filthier about the rot he was now into. He was betraying his team, his country and, above all, his conscience. Would he ever be the same man again?

Random thoughts flooded his mind as the beer began to take effect. He would call a press conference and announce his retirement. No...that wouldn't help. The slimeball would still post the pictures and videos online. He would still be ruined... the name and fame built over the years, gone...That wouldn't do...wouldn't do at all.

As fitful sleep was beginning to settle over his tired body and mind, his eyes fell on the phone. Before drifting away, he made a mental note to change that gaudy ringtone sometime soon.

15

Mohali

It was increasingly evident to the think tank that going into the next game at Mohali without a revised strategy would be a sure fire recipe for disaster. The steadily increasing number of practice sessions I was being subjected to made me think that I would feature somewhere in their plans. But how greatly the team's attitude towards me had thawed became clear only when a highly untoward incident occurred.

I was in the middle of a good spell in which I had caught Giri in two minds on a number of occasions. Suddenly Yaj walked in, all padded up, and requested Giri to step away from the crease. As I stood at the top of my mark, the puzzled look on my face could be seen a mile away. Yaj took a middle stump guard and then wandered down the pitch to do a spot of gardening. Then, he casually swaggered his way to the crease and eased into his classical stance. For a fleeting second, our eyes met and I thought I detected the faintest of nods. Was that an olive branch?

I raced down the track and let one rip. Yaj swung wild and missed it by a mile, while the ball missed timber by an inch. A collective 'oooh' escaped the crowd that had gathered to witness some fireworks, given the history between us. I must assume that they were thoroughly disappointed, because all that Yaj said was, 'Well bowled, Nick.'

I am usually good at hiding my feelings, but I simply couldn't mask the absolute incredulity that clouded my face at that instant. Here was a guy who had been avoiding me like the plague ever since that fateful day in Bangalore! I knew for a fact that Bill, though he would be loath to admit it, had been doctoring the training schedules so I never got to bowl at Yaj in the nets. And here he was, voluntarily walking out to face me, and even shouting out encouragement.

Unsure how to react, I walked back to the mark. I then proceeded to bowl what commentators love to describe as a 'probing spell' and was pleased to note that I could still make Yaj jump around like a cat-on-a-hot-tin-roof.

Throughout the spell, Yaj's perplexing behaviour continued. He played and missed on numerous occasions, was bowled twice and, in a near repeat of the Bangalore incident, took a knock to the helmet as well. Through this ordeal, our man admirably demonstrated how to grin-and-bear-it. The steady stream of encouragement flowed relentless.

At the end of it all, he shook me by the hand and even suggested we have a drink together later that evening. In short, it looked like he was making a genuine attempt at making amends for the past and that sometime in the near future the possibility of the two of us getting along like a house on fire could not be ruled out.

The day before our second game in the series dawned in this better light. At breakfast, Monty read out the names of the playing eleven in the order in which they were to bat. The eleventh name he read out was mine.

My day had come! There were congratulatory pats and handshakes all along. In keeping with our newfound friendship, Yaj walked over and gave me a hug.

The only sour note was that I had replaced my good friend Guru, the champion offspinner. That too, in a game to be played on his home ground. The logic floating around was that Mohali was traditionally a fast bowler's paradise and spinners could be taken for a lot of runs. But deep inside, we all knew that the man was being hung out to dry for having had an ordinary outing in the Kotla game. Also, the think tank was confining the two spinner theory to the deep freezer and swapping it for a three-pronged seam attack.

If anything, Mohali was far more picturesque than Kotla. With its newly laid canopied roof, vast stretches of open stands and the unusual number of eight floodlight towers, the ground was a rare blend of old world charm with the delights of the modern game. Disappointment at not playing my first game in New Delhi gave way to elation at making my debut on this fantastic ground.

I called my parents to give them the glad tidings, thereby handing mom a chance to sob over a STD call. Some semblance of order was restored when Dad came online, but even in his voice, I could detect a treble that in his case spoke of a particularly nasty case of heightened emotions.

I spoke to Bonsai too, and once more enquired after Nisha. No news, which in this case was not exactly good news. Where was that girl? And why was I still feeling a pang each time she came to mind, which, by the way, was often.

I reeled when I read the headlines in the newspaper on the morning of the big game, 'India to unleash secret lethal weapon on the Pakistanis'. They made it sound like we were planning to dump nerve gas on the men from across the border. I cannot deny experiencing an initial heady feeling, which lasted a few minutes, only to be replaced by an icy-cold one that took up residence in the region comprising the heart, stomach and possibly one kidney.

How I wished then that my entry into world cricket had been an unheralded affair! I do not remember experiencing the load of expectations to this degree since I was expected to breeze through the multiplication table of four upon successfully having demonstrated my potential by memorising that nursery rhyme in my third grade.

I cannot even begin to describe the pride I felt upon donning Team India colours for the first time. Therefore, I shall not attempt it. I proudly bore the number forty-two on my back, in tribute to my favourite author, Douglas Adams. I deliberated on whether I should have the name 'Hariharan' on my jersey, but abandoned the idea because it bought amusing pictures of an old man ambling in to bowl to mind. Eventually, I settled for Nikhil.

16

Comply or Perish

*H*e fumbled with his kit in the dressing room, lost in thought, even as his teammates prepared to walk out for the rendering of the national anthem. The atmosphere in the room was charged and he felt a gut-wrenching, sick feeling in his stomach. Was he really about to betray this bunch? Again? He knew the answer almost as soon as the question popped in his head. He did not have a choice. The early morning conversation with Noor had put the issue beyond doubt in his mind. Comply or perish. Those were the only two options he had.

He had succeeded in his task in New Delhi. He would get his opportunity here as well, but the trouble would be to pull it off without arousing any suspicion. It would take a miracle to pull this one off. To make matters worse, he had not had a chance to privately speak to the stooge Noor had identified. God knows he had gone out of his way to get friendly with that bloke, but the bugger had proven more slippery than an eel.

Noor had expressed his disapproval of the lack of progress on that front in no uncertain terms. He had insisted on the sheer importance of bringing the guy around because the task was too big to be accomplished single-handed. As if he didn't know! When this ordeal was finally over and he had all the dirty material safe in his hands, he would strangle Noor with his bare hands. The thought made him smile.

The younger members of the team were straining at the leash like a pack of dogs, impatient to step out. When the time came, they led the way, while he and some of the more senior members of the team brought up the rear. His eyes were focused on the rookies in the vanguard. Suddenly, he saw one of them turn sharply to look at a girl in the crowd, who had been dancing around and screaming his name to get his attention. 'Idiot,' he thought, 'does he even know what lies in store? That chick must be his girlfriend.' Suddenly, part of an earlier conversation with Noor flashed through his head—*I have made arrangements to get his girl here...*

17

Baptism by Fire

$\mathscr{I}$ had turned sharply upon hearing a familiar voice yell out my name. I couldn't believe my eyes! It was Nisha; she was standing with a group of spectators that had lined up along the steps leading from the dressing room to the ground. For a moment, I stared at her as if I had seen a ghost. Then, before my senses could recover, I was pushed along by my colleagues. 'I'll wait for you,' she mouthed and blew me a kiss.

'How the hell did she get here?' was the fundamental question in my mind at that moment, but I realized that I was way too happy to care anyway. The important thing was that she had come and suddenly all the disappointment and frustration at not having heard from her for over a month evaporated.

The newspaper that had carried a mugshot of mine after the Kotla game, which made the Grim Reaper look happy as a lark, carried one the next day that had me grinning from ear to ear like a certified idiot. The grin was only partly due to the patriotism that caroused through my veins as I heard the national anthem rendered and the tricolour hoisted. I think the presence of one particular girl in the stands had quite a lot to do with it as well.

Like for all games, the team's think tank comprising the captain and senior pros such as Vijay, Giri, Guru, Yaj and Roshan, had worked out a plan for this one as well. For the first time since I joined the team, I had been invited to the meetings where this plan was hatched. Part of the plan was to bowl first upon winning the toss and to start with Ash and I, the theory being that the Pakistanis would not expect a rookie and an offspinner to operate with the new ball.

I started to warm up as soon as Monty won the toss and put the opposition in on a wicket that looked fresh and new. I was relishing the prospect of making first use of it. I thought it had been rather generous of Roshan to concede the new ball to me, especially considering the bad blood between us. Like with Yaj, I had noticed a considerable thawing of the frost between Roshan and me. He was not yet exactly approachable, but he wasn't biting either.

I will never forget the moment I stepped on the turf for the first time for as long as I live. Clichéd as it sounds, time really did stop still for that moment. Amidst the deafening roar reverberating from the throats of thousands of fans in the stadium, my captain handed me my first cap. I was finally an Indian cricketer. Twelve years after a boy of eight had dreamt this dream, a man of twenty was seeing it fulfilled.

In the previous game, I had had the privilege of watching a few battles being waged out in the centre. To now move from that passive role into the thick of the battle was a huge paradigm shift for me. I noticed how the picturesque stadium that I had admired from the safety of the dressing room, took on menacing proportions now that I was out in the middle. Thousands and thousands of fans, waving banners, posters, flags and placards took on the form of bloodthirsty spectators in the Coliseum, baying for the blood of the gladiators.

Salim and Khaled, the Pakistani opening pair walked out into the middle. A huge contingent of Pakistani supporters had crossed the Wagah Border into Chandigarh over the last couple of days. As a result, Mohali was bathed in blue and green in equal measure. At Delhi, the Pakistanis had smelt blood. They were confident that their team would move in for the kill at Chandigarh.

I was now thoroughly warmed up but also nervous as hell. There were butterflies the size of bats in my stomach. I saw the umpire handing the brand new Kookaburra to Monty and started walking towards him. To my amazement, Monty tossed the ball to Roshan. I was banished to long off without as much as an explanation. I looked in the direction of Vijay, who was stationed at first slip. He had a quizzical expression on his face as well. Catching my eye, he shrugged, almost helplessly. Clearly, the man had been caught off guard by the sudden change in plan as much as I had.

Since there was not much that I could do, I swallowed my disappointment and went off to the boundary to play my part as one of two fielders outside the inner circle for the first ten overs of the game. Roshan bowled a good first over, towards the end of which, a fleeting hope of getting to bowl the second over from the other end had started germinating in my mind. This was nipped in the bud when Monty tossed the ball to Shiv. I couldn't figure out what was happening. Why was Ash not given the other new ball as planned? Was there a change in strategy at the last minute? Why wasn't I told about it? Then the depressing thoughts began to set in. Perhaps I am too small a fry to be privy to such matters! My confidence graph went into a spiraling nosedive.

Even as these thoughts gnawed at my mind, I had my first piece of action on the cricket field. A booming drive from the blade of Khaled beat the infield and made its way to the boundary about ten yards to my left. I easily covered the ground, collected the ball cleanly and rocketed it into the gloves of the keeper in one smooth, strong action. It was no great shakes, really, any professional cricketer worth his salt would have been expected to do that in his sleep. But the thrill of having the crowd root for you is indescribable. I felt like I was on top of the world and my confidence pulled out of the nosedive just seconds before it crashed.

Admittedly, Roshan and Shiv did a reasonable job with the new ball this time. They kept things tight, but the breakthrough was not exactly forthcoming. I could only wonder if things would have been different had we stuck to our original plan.

Ash took over as first change, replacing Shiv in the twelfth over of the innings. By then, both batsmen had their eye in and were seeing the ball as big as a football, as commentators loved to say. Roshan bowled two more overs from his end.

I had never seen him bowl such a marathon spell, without doing much more than beat the bat on a couple of occasions. I wondered why Monty had allowed him to go on for so long, but then dismissed the thought as a negative reaction to the disappointment I was feeling.

When Vijay came on to replace Roshan in the seventeenth over, my head dropped in resignation. Monty had chosen a part-timer ahead of his frontline bowler! Were we reverting to some version of the two-spinner theory again after having thoroughly analysed and abandoned it? Like so many times in my life, I just didn't know what to think.

Around the twenty-third over, with the Pakistanis sitting comfortably on 112/0, Salim mishit a Vijay longhop in my direction. For a heart-stopping second, I lost the ball in the crowd, before it suddenly reappeared in my field of vision. I sprinted towards the ball and lunged full length. The ball fell short by an agonising inch, but nestled safely in my palms on the bounce as I took a tumble. Thanks to the momentum I had gathered running towards the ball, the tumble ended with me upright on my feet, ready to fire the ball in.

The non-striker, as he is sometimes bound to do when confronted with such an 'iffy' moment, had been ball watching while his partner had turned blind for a second run. In the end, that moment's hesitation cost them dearly. Khaled, after having gaped open-mouthed at my acrobatics, recovered his senses and hared down the pitch to the non-striker's end. I took aim and let rip, watching incredulously as Vijay nearly tried to collect the ball in front of the stumps, before pulling his hands out of harm's way at the last moment and letting it crash into the timber.

The third umpire was called for, even as my teammates rushed towards me, clapping my back and tousling my hair. The TV replays showed that the batsman had been just short of the crease sending us into a wild frenzy of celebration. My first real contribution to the team's cause was not with the ball or the bat, but on the field. I was simply too busy basking in the glory to be complaining.

'Sorry, dude,' said Vijay, slipping a hand around my shoulder. 'I nearly killed it! It was bloody instinctive that I stuck my hand out. I'm glad I pulled out or that one would have ripped my arm off.'

'Hey, no problem Vijay. I would have probably attempted the same,' I said, more to cover the embarrassment of a senior apologizing to a rank rookie, than because I believed I would have done something that stupid. 'By the way, do you think I am gonna have a bowl anytime soon? Monty seems to have forgotten I exist and am actually not a substitute for this game.'

'Yeah, buddy…I have no clue what's going on or why we are moving away from that elaborate plan we had worked out. I've been in his ear right from ball one, but the skipper seems to have hatched a new plan while we were sleeping. Anyway, he has been known to spring surprises like this in the past and it has often worked. But I think you should get warmed up.'

I saw Vijay walk to Monty and talk animatedly, like I had seen him do all day long. Monty nodded and gestured to me to take the ball. Good old Vijay had pulled it for me! Finally, my chance to bowl had come, albeit twenty-four overs later than originally scheduled.

18

All Dressed Up and Nowhere to Go

*M*y stint in the field and the run-out I had orchestrated had made me forget the butterflies in my stomach temporarily. As I handed my sunhat to the umpire and marked my runup, they were back, bigger and stronger than before.

I mouthed a silent prayer and thought of Mom and Dad. I knew they'd be watching and praying for me. I thought of Nisha, which was not surprising. Then I thought of Mishra Aunty, my hug-happy neighbour from the past, which was very surprising, and a clear sign that my mind was drifting and I was losing focus.

So this is how it felt! Big occasion, historic stadium, full-throated cheering from thirty-thousand fans, your teammates egging you on…and yet there cannot be a greater moment of solitude than when you are at the top of your runup, waiting to bowl that first ball.

You dream of this moment all your life, hoping against hope that it would be something as miraculous as a first ball wicket, while praying it wouldn't be something as inauspicious as a no-ball or a wide. In the event, my first ball settled for the 'in-between' between these two extremes. I dished out a full-length, almost juicy half volley on middle and off, which most batsmen would have pounced upon with delight. Thankfully, in my case, the batsman was new to the crease and he chose to play it safe, defending it quietly into the offside. It was like a monkey was off my back. As the over progressed, I found my rhythm settling in and consequently the pace picking up a few notches with every delivery.

My first over was a statistical rarity in limited overs cricket—a maiden. Although I did bowl accurately, I think the lack of runs was primarily because the new batsman was biding his time to settle in.

I nearly got another monkey off my back when in my third over I bowled a snorter of a delivery that kicked from good length, took the shoulder of the bat, and flew towards point. Yaj, normally the safest of hands, moved a fraction too late to his left and spilt the chance. My hands flew to my head, but I quickly managed to hide my frustration.

Two overs down the line, this particular little monkey had grown to the size of a gorilla. I was bowling quick, almost 90 plus mph, but without luck. The ball was refusing to swing and the pitch was still too good to get any serious movement off it.

At the drinks break, the Pakistanis were placed at a comfortable 155/1 and we were staring down the proverbial barrel. Monty called an emergency meeting of the troops. 'Guys, we need to really pull a rabbit out of the hat now. I am gonna get Roshan back on. I was hoping to hold him back for the slog overs, but looks like I have no choice.'

'Monty, let me have a go for a couple of overs,' Yaj volunteered. 'I think they are expecting either Roshan or Shiv to come on. They may just get excited enough to play big shots and commit hara-kiri when they see me.'

To me, it seemed like a sound idea for two reasons. Firstly, the logic was good. It did look like the batsmen were readying to have a go at the bowling. And, usually, a drinks break brought about a lapse in concentration. Secondly, nothing else seemed to be working, so we might as well give it a shot. Yaj's persistence finally paid off and Monty agreed to bring him on.

After the drinks break, therefore, Monty pressed a third spinner into action. Yaj's first over cost ten runs. To be fair to the man, at least a part of his theory that the batsmen would be happy to see him was accurate. In fact, the batsmen couldn't believe their luck at the dollies he was dishing out.

A measure of the happiness the batsmen felt could be gauged by the three sixes that a rampaging Salim smashed in Yaj's next over. Then he got carried away and attempted a fourth one over long on, a shot that would have taken him to a well-deserved hundred. But in doing so, he top-edged the ball and it flew towards long off, where yours truly was stationed.

For the second time that day, I momentarily lost the ball in the crowd. Instinctively, I moved forward. This time, when the ball appeared, I realized that I had overshot it by a fair distance and now had no option but to throw myself backward, hoping the ball would stick. As the ball descended, I loped backwards and threw myself, right hand outstretched. I felt the thud of the ball slamming into my palm a second before I felt the thud of my body hitting the ground.

Looking at the replay of that catch on the giant screen, even as my team gathered around, I realized that I had made a simple catch look difficult. Had I just stood my ground, and not moved about like a guy high on a couple of stiff drinks, the ball would have literally fallen into my lap. But, admittedly, it looked spectacular on the big screen and, most importantly, I had held on to it, though my body was sore for the next five overs thanks to the fall.

The Yaj experiment was canned after that. Two overs from the man had earned us a wicket but at a whopping cost of twenty-eight runs! With the score at 190/2 after the thirty-fifth over, I was brought back for a second spell. My figures so far read five overs, one maiden, eighteen runs, and no wickets. It was the last mentioned bit of statistics that I was keen to rectify.

Since two different balls were being used from either end, they were each only about eighteen overs old. Looking at the ball in my hand, I noticed how scuffed one side was. The lights were also beginning to take effect. I knew that if I bowled all out, the ball would reverse swing.

Cricket is so full of these double entendres, or at least of phrases that leave you a little flabbergasted. For instance, 'Do you swing it both ways?' is not a questioning of the sexual orientation of the questioned, but a perfectly normal way of asking if the person in question can move the ball both ways. Similarly, 'reverse swing' is also not a euphemism for deviant sexual behaviour of any kind. As an invention, the art of reverse swing is attributed to a great Pakistani pace duo of the nineties. Although it was probably already known to the West Indies Greats of previous decades and to Dennis Lillee and Jeff Thompson, it was the legendary Ws of Pakistan that really exploited the art to great effect.

The cricket ball is designed to swing. Fielders who are usually seen busily polishing one side of the ball do so to 'maintain the shine'. When a pace bowler bowls a cricket ball that is shinier on one side than on the other, the ball tends to deviate towards the shiny side. Reverse swing is the very opposite of this phenomenon. When the ball grows old, it tends to swing towards the rougher side, thoroughly confusing the batsmen, who are used to playing conventional swing.

It was this aerodynamic principle that I was hoping to find and exploit.

'Find' I did with the very first ball, but 'exploit' I didn't. The batsman, Salman Rashid, misread the swing and played the ball in the air through midwicket, where Vijay dropped a sitter. The ball popped out, like toast out of a toaster. I buried my face in despair, an expression that was mirrored by a distraught Vijay.

However, I didn't have to wait much longer for my first taste of success. Two balls later, I bowled a reverse swinging toe crusher and was rewarded with the crashing sound of the ball hitting timber. Finally, the gorilla was off my back and I had joined the long list of people who could boast of having at least one wicket to their name in international cricket.

I pumped my fist in celebration. Looking up at the giant screen, I was amazed to see Nisha's face show up. I'm not sure if it was sheer coincidence or whether some cameraman, having witnessed our brief encounter before the match, had deliberately sought her out and focused on her. But the fact of the matter was that a roving camera had focused on her at the precise moment I took my first wicket and captured her leaping up in pure, unadulterated joy.

Like it so often happens, success begets success. I managed to bag three more wickets before downing the shutters for the day. My second came via a caught behind, the third fell leg before to another reverse swinging yorker and the fourth was caught at long on, while attempting to slog the ball out of the park. While I felt pleased to have bowled reasonably well on debut, I also realized that the batsmen had helped me by playing far too many adventurous shots.

We were right back in the game. From a commanding 200/2 in the thirty-seventh over, the Pakistanis had collapsed to 243/7 by the end of the forty-fourth. My four wickets had come at the cost of forty-one runs, returns that I would settle for any day of the week, month or year for the rest of my cricketing career.

The three remaining batsmen added a further twenty runs between them before the Pakistanis shut shop at a score of 263 inside fifty overs. As targets go, this was eminently achievable, but our batting form from the last game not being exactly confidence-inducing, the atmosphere in the dressing room was suitably subdued. We just made sure that Vijay did not attempt any shadow batting this time.

When the established firm of Gupta and Sehgal took up opening duties, their approach was a far cry from the flamboyant stuff they were used to dishing out. Vijay seemed to have deliberately cut down all risky shots and looked set for the long haul. The first ten overs only produced thirty-six runs, with Vijay getting sixteen off thirty-two balls! The great news was that we had all our wickets intact.

This, however, was set to change. After the pair had put on fifty in fifteen overs, Vijay played his first aggressive shot of the evening. The ball flew to the left of the sweeper guarding the midwicket boundary. Vijay called Giri for the second and charged down the wicket. Half way down the pitch, however, he seemed to change his mind, screamed out a loud 'No' and scampered back to the non-striker's end. Even though Giri was far too committed, he made a lionhearted effort to turn back, but was not quick enough to beat the throw from the rope. As Giri made the long trek back to the hut, the lingering image of a downcast Vijay on his knees at the non-striker's end filled the giant screen.

To his credit, the error in judgment did not seem to have affected Vijay's concentration. If anything, he was focusing even more intently. However, he seemed shaken up by the incident and from then on his timing went for a toss.

Monty, the compulsive gambler, promoted Yaj up the order at one-down, with the intention of upping the scoring rate and continuing the 'unsettling' left-hand-right-hand combination in the middle.

Unsettling it certainly was…not to the Pakistanis, but to us sitting in the pavilion watching two of our champs struggling to come to terms with some quality fast bowling as well as each other. So outrageous was the running between the wickets that it seemed like they were conjuring up innovative ways of running each other out. Each time they escaped by the proverbial skins of their respective dentures, they initiated urgent mid-pitch conferences, followed by a lot of glove thumping...but these antics didn't seem to be doing much good.

While these legends were handing out free lessons on how to commit suicide out there in the middle, the runs were drying up faster than municipal taps in summer. The asking rate was now more like a 'demanding' rate and steadily progressing towards double figures.

The pair played out twenty overs between them, scoring eighty-two runs. At the end of the thirty-eighth over, our score was 132/1. Vijay was crawling to the most painstaking fifty of his career and Yaj looked like he'd shed grateful tears for the mere privilege of being able to put bat to ball. To win, we needed to double that score in twelve overs at the rate of exactly eleven runs per over.

At that point, the enormity of the task seemed to have finally sunk into the mind of one of our sleeping beauties. Yaj suddenly and quite inexplicably seemed to have found some form and opened out with a flurry of strokes, before playing one shot too many and holing out to the fielder in the deep. After forty overs, we were 152/2 and needed to score one hundred and twelve off sixty balls.

A sense of real urgency seemed to descend upon the entire team. Cameos by Viraj, Roshan, Rana and Monty pushed the score to 244/6 at the end of the forty-eighth. The target was now twenty off twelve, achievable mainly because our slumbering giant, Vijay, was still out there. But he was running out of partners as Ash and Roshan fell in rapid succession. When Shiv walked in to join him in the forty-ninth over, we still needed thirteen runs off three balls and the one batsman left in the hut was a rookie making his international debut!

In the end, I just sat there in the pavilion, all dressed up and nowhere to go. I never made the walk to the middle that evening. After the last ball had been bowled, we were seven runs short and my debut game had ended in a heart-shattering loss.

19

Judas

That evening, we received a thorough dressing down in the dressing room. My efforts with the ball and in the field were understandably buried in the aftermath of our disastrous show with the bat. We sat through the post-match analysis like zombies. Vijay and Yaj came for some extra-special treatment. How could they crawl through the powerplay overs? Both were experienced players with well established, aggressive styles. What caused them to deviate from the norm?

I could sense my roommate's state of mind. He had sleepwalked through the innings, trying desperately to put bat to ball. He had clearly had an off day, as everyone had a right to occasionally. I thought that Monty was not being fair in zeroing down on Vijay and Yaj as the villains of the match. I felt he had a big hand in it as well, starting with the mindboggling decision to change the game strategy at the onset. Someone raised this point in the meeting, leading to a heated argument. Before any clear conclusions could be drawn, Bill decided to step in and call it a day. It was clear that our brains were too numb and fatigued to take in any more analysis.

The storm clouds were beginning to gather overhead again. In all this, Nisha was like the proverbial silver lining. She had called after the match and we had arranged to meet at ten.

When I reached the restaurant, she was not there. Memories of another restaurant and a broken promise were just returning to haunt me, when she entered, looking breathtaking in a black dress.

We ordered our drinks and settled down on a plush sofa in a corner. She smiled and lay one hand on mine. 'Congratulations, Nick…on a wonderful debut.'

'Thanks,' I smiled back. 'I wish it had been a little better. I wish we had won.' A cloud seemed to pass over her face.

Our drinks arrived and we raised a toast to our friendship.

'Where did you disappear, Nish?'

'Nick…I'm sorry I had to go that way. I just couldn't tell you.'

'You couldn't have called?'

'I'm sorry,' she said, taking a sip of her drink. 'Nick, I have a confession to make.'

I nearly choked on my drink.

'I haven't been entirely honest with you.'

'Wait,' I said, my heart shattering in a million anticipatory pieces, 'Let me guess. Are you and Gaurav seeing each other?'

'What? WHAT? No, you moron! Whatever made you think that?'

I took a big gulp of my drink and actually choked.

'No, you dumb-ass. It's something else. Look, I need you to swear that no one else is to know what I'm going to tell you now.'

'Cross my heart, hope to die,' I said, delirious with relief.

'I'm investigating something for the paper. That's why I'm here.'

'Oh!' I said weakly, 'I thought...'

'What?'

'Nothing. You were saying?'

'Are you drunk?' she asked, eyeing me suspiciously, 'Like I was saying, I'm here investigating something for my paper... something that could have serious repercussions for your team, especially if I smoke someone out.'

It was my turn to wonder if she was drunk!

'Nick, do you think something was not quite right about today's game?'

'Er...yeah. We lost. That didn't seem quite right.'

'No, you ass, I don't mean that. Do you think someone was not putting in a hundred per cent?'

'You must be kidding, Nish. This is Team India we are talking about. Everyone pulls his weight and gives a hundred per cent all the time.'

She sighed. 'I wouldn't be so sure of that. In my job, I have heard stuff that would make your stomach turn. Let me come to the point. I think there is a traitor in the team, who has sold out to a bookie. He is tanking games and betraying the team and country.'

'Nish, you must be out of your mind. I know these guys.

They will give an arm, a leg and a few other vital organs if that is what it takes to win this series. Just because we lost a couple of games, doesn't mean something dirty is going on.'

'Do you think I will say something like this without being sure?'

'Sure? You are sure about this?'

'Reasonably sure.'

'That's no good, Nish. You can't drag somebody through mud just because you are "reasonably sure" he is up to something.'

'If my investigation turns up nothing, or helps clear someone's name, believe me Nick, there would be no one happier than me. However, if there is a traitor in your midst, we must do everything in our power to find him and stop him.'

I wasn't sure I liked the sound of that 'we'. What did she mean 'we'?

'I need your help, Nick. I need to get close to the team. You are the only one who can help me do that. I need to watch and observe. I need to collect evidence, if there is any. We don't have much time, Nick. That man, if he exists, will eat the team from the inside and before you know it, your series would be over. Your career could be finished just because of one man's greed.'

Eventually, the inevitable happened. I let her talk me into becoming an accomplice in her grand plans of apprehending 'Judas', as we codenamed the alleged traitor.

20

A Close Shave!

*H*e wasn't exactly tossing or turning in his bed, but sleep simply wouldn't come. The gut-wrenching disgust he felt following the game was still there, but the intensity was on a far lesser scale. Two games he had cost his team. One more and that would be the end of the series for India. His mind wandered to the game that had ended just hours earlier. It had been tough to get the team to deviate from the originally decided strategy and the personal risk involved had been substantial. The batting fiasco had been better orchestrated. The vein of bad batting form running through most of the top and middle order had effectively masked his sabotaging role.

Suddenly, the cell phone rang and he froze as he heard his roommate stir. Grabbing the phone, he dashed into the washroom and locked the door. He sat on the pot and answered the call.

'You are taking longer to answer my call each time, my friend. I sometimes worry what might happen if I get trigger-happy and upload your video on YouTube, just because you didn't pick my call in time!'

Cornered as he was, he still knew that Noor would do nothing of that sort. The arrangement was working too perfectly for him to want to kill the goose. So, when he replied, there was a rare streak of confidence in his voice. 'Noor, let's cut the crap and get down to the business. Why did you call me at this hour of the night? Don't you know that my roommate would be here as well?'

'Some things just can't wait, my friend. First, accept my congratulations on a superb job done. I always knew you were the right man for the job and you have just repaid my trust. Well done!'

He controlled his rising fury with enormous effort. 'I'm all ears, Noor.'

'Good! Now listen to me. One more game and we are done. If India loses this one, I'll call off the arrangement and then you can really go out and enjoy the two other inconsequential games. How does that sound?'

He closed his eyes, unable to answer. It sounded sick! That's how it sounded.

'You there?'

'Yes,' he managed.

'For a moment I thought I had lost you there. Listen, how's the progress with that other guy you were to talk to? Have you gotten in touch with him?'

'I haven't, Noor. I tried, but I just have not been able to

speak to him alone.'

'Well, you've got to move fast, buddy. It is always nice to have another mule to do that dirty work along with you. It will surely help mask your efforts.' The ugly cackle filled his ear and he hurriedly held the phone away.

He heard the phone go dead and leant against the flush tank. Then he rose weakly and opened the door of the washroom. The sight he saw made his heart leap to his mouth. Standing near the door, looking only slightly groggy, was his roommate.

Quick as a flash, he slipped the phone into his pocket. His roommate didn't seem to have noticed it.

'Hey,' he said, trying to keep his voice steady, 'what are you doing up so late?'

'I thought I heard you talking in the washroom.'

'Me? In the washroom? Why would I do that?'

'Well, I thought I heard something. You sounded angry.'

'You are too tired. That's why you are hearing things. I'm going to sleep. See you in the morning. Good night.' He slid under his blanket and pretended to sleep.

His roommate stood for a few seconds, watching him. As he entered the washroom, the thought in his mind was, 'Why does he have such a cheap cell phone?'

21

Mission Inside Edge

$\mathscr{U}$nlike his predecessors, Bill had a liberal attitude towards the WAGS of the team mucking around with their husbands or boyfriends, as the case may be. Of course, he wouldn't hear of them staying together, but a little bit of socialising after games he wasn't averse to. In fact, he openly encouraged it, saying that it would help the team unwind a little and be more relaxed to take on the battles ahead.

It was this attitude that Nisha decided to exploit to the hilt to get close to the team and try to identify the rotten apple. My teammates had seen the kiss she had blown my way as I walked down the stairs to the ground the other day. They had seen her dance like crazy when I took that first wicket, courtesy the official broadcasters and the giant screen. A few also remembered the 'pretty girl' who had accompanied me that fateful day I had bowled that spell to Yaj in Bangalore.

So, introducing her to the team as my 'girlfriend' was a piece of cake.

Our next game was at the most historic ground in the country, the Eden Gardens in Kolkata.

The boys seemed to have put the loss in the previous game behind them and their hearts and souls into the practice sessions the day before the game. The upcoming encounter was a 'do-or-die' situation. Although the form of most of our batsmen and quite a few of our bowlers was suspect, the think tank refused to tinker too much with the lineup. The only change made was to bring Guru in place of fellow offie, Ash.

I met Nisha at a quiet little coffee shop the evening before the game. After placing our orders, she produced a notepad and pen. On the first page of the notepad, she wrote something in big bold letters and showed it to me.

I read it aloud, 'Mission Inside Edge.'

'Yes,' she said, with a self-satisfied air. 'Mission Inside Edge.'

'Nice beginning,' I said. 'What next?'

'I think we should go about our task in an ordered way. Let's begin by creating a list of suspects. Who do you think has been performing suspiciously, Nick? Give me a frank opinion.'

This was a stumper of a question. While I could easily think of a number of substandard performances that we had put up so far in the series, I struggled to think of any of them as 'suspicious'. After racking my brains for quite a while, I reluctantly put down a name on the pad.

'Yaj?' she asked, reading aloud, 'are you sure you are not simply being biased?'

Now this was rich! First, the woman asks for a frank

opinion and then counters the very first one I offer!

'Well, he hasn't done well at all in any of the games we have played so far,' I said, defensively.

'Ok, let us put his name down. If nothing else, we at least have something to start with.'

'You've been watching the games yourself. Why don't you put a name down?'

'Hmm...how about Ash?'

'Ash? He has been the only bowler performing reasonably consistently.'

'So why is he out of tomorrow's game, then?'

We looked at each other silently for a few seconds, pondering this question. Then, she picked up the pencil and wrote Monty's name on the list. Would Monty, the hero of the nation, commit such a dastardly crime? 'But,' I thought aloud, 'his actions have been suspicious. Why did he change the game plan without letting any of us in on it? Even someone as senior as Vijay had been kept in the dark.'

'And Vijay?'

'Nisha, Vijay is clearly out of form. Think like a bookie. If you pick a guy to fix matches for you, you want him to throw away his wicket...not stick around to the very end in a desperate attempt to win a game. And he was in Monty's ears the entire game today, trying to make the man see sense and revert to the original game plan.'

'How about Roshan, then?' Nisha asked.

'He has been inconsistent. Could that be a sign that something's fishy?'

She wrote down Roshan's name on the list.

We racked our brains over the next half hour, but couldn't go beyond the names we had zeroed-in on. Many names were considered, but I vetoed most of them. I read the list over once, trying to gather my thoughts. I wasn't very comfortable with having helped put my teammates on the suspects' list, but I knew I had provided an honest appraisal.

Nisha had made sure we discussed everyone, including me. I was let off the hook because she considered me a little too wet-behind-the-ears to be of any use to bookies. She conveniently ignored the fact that I had only played one game and had actually done well in that and was, therefore, automatically above suspicion.

In spite of its newly acquired grandeur and decidedly more aesthetic looks, the Eden Gardens was far from the most awe-inspiring sights in world cricket. But what was undeniable was the immense cricketing history associated with this ground. Who could forget the famous Hero Cup victory, followed by the memorable sight of the entire stadium shining in the light of the thousands of placards that the cricket-crazy Kolkatans had burned to mark the occasion? Would anyone who had witnessed the heroics of VVS Laxman and Dravid against the Aussies in 2001 ever forget it? These were the legends that boys like me all over the country had been brought up on. To us, the Eden Gardens was far greater than the Lords', the MCGs, and the SCGs of the world put together.

I had had my taste of what it is like to play in front of thousands of spectators. But nothing really prepared me for Kolkata. From the petrified look on the face of the Pakistanis, I could sense that nothing had prepared them for it either.

Though we were 2-0 down in the series, I sensed that we would go into this game as champions.

Not surprisingly, Monty chose to bowl on winning the toss. Some experts see this as a negative move, but no captain in his right mind would want to lose an opportunity to exploit the early juice in the wicket. It was now up to our spearheads to make the early inroads into the Pakistani lineup.

While I had expected to make it to the playing eleven, I had clearly not anticipated that my skipper would let me make first use of the new ball. The 'Master of the Sensational' that he was, the guy had thought it fit to let me in on the big secret only after he had won the toss, elected to field and we were about fifteen minutes from the start of play.

The Pakistanis came out breathing fire. Khaled and Salim creamed us all over the park in the first five overs. In the sixth over, my third of the afternoon, Khaled paid the price for throwing caution to the wind and ended up spooning a catch to the sole fielder out on the fence on the offside. I was pleased to note the considerable bounce in the pitch that had induced the mistake from the seasoned campaigner.

With the very next ball, I trapped the Pakistani skipper Rashid Khan plumb in front. I was super convinced that I had my man, but had to agonise through a third umpire review before the decision was confirmed and the skipper got his marching orders.

So there I was, playing just my second game and on a hattrick. In theory, I knew what I had to do. After all, hadn't I heard TV commentators coach bowlers, who couldn't exactly hear them, how to go about getting hattricks? All I had to do was bowl nice and full.

I didn't get the hattrick. I bowled nice and full, but the batsman kept the ball out. But the good part was that we had derailed their train off its tracks and from then on, the momentum swung our way.

I didn't do much more in that game, other than watch with satisfaction as the famed Pakistani lineup folded for a total of 226. We now had a real sniff.

Unfortunately, our champion was yet to rediscover his sublime touch. Vijay didn't exactly potter around this time. In fact, he didn't last long enough to potter around. Fortunately, another champion chose this precise moment to stand up and be counted. Yaj, my hero-turned-nemesis-turned-friend-again, and the top favourite Judas contender on our list, sauntered to the middle with a Viv Richardesque swagger, exuding a confidence I had not seen in a long time. That confidence translated into a superlative performance that blew the Pakistanis away and earned us our first win in the series. The World Champions were hanging in there and perhaps just beginning to turn things around.

The win lifted our spirits even though deep in our hearts we knew we were not out of the woods, yet. There was the ever-looming issue of the woeful form of our openers, our middle order was about as reliable as the weather report, our bowlers were not exactly striking terror in the hearts of batsmen and our fielders weren't exactly setting the field on fire. But with a win securely under our belts, we carried a semblance of confidence into our next game in Ahmedabad.

22

I Find an Ally

$\mathcal{B}$y the end of the Kolkata game, Nisha still held on to her belief that either Roshan or Yaj was the black sheep in the flock. An explanation as to why no others had made their way into the list wasn't exactly forthcoming. Honestly, I didn't care to know either and was secretly glad to have that many lesser numbers to spy on. Many times I tried to tell her that this James Bond thingy wasn't exactly my kind of thingy, and that she should get a professional to do the snooping. But you know how girls can be, especially when their minds are set upon something. And this particular girl had clearly set her mind upon smoking out the vermin from this underground lair and I was to be the bait!

Apparently, the espionage wasn't restricted to some old fashioned Mata Hari stuff alone. There were gadgets that would have made James Bond nod with approval to be involved too.

'Here,' she said, pulling out what looked, at first sight, like a tube of lipstick from her purse.

'What do I do with this…lipstick?'

'Give it to Yaj.'

'You want me…to give this…lipstick…to Yaj?'

'That is a highly sophisticated recording device, you moron.'

'Very impressive! But I will still look very silly handing it to Yaj, don't you think?'

'You don't "hand" it to him. Just place it somewhere in his room where it can catch any audio signals.'

'And how do I do that?'

'I don't know. Think of something…Do I have to think of everything?'

No, she did not have to think of everything. But I would have really appreciated some help this time. How on earth was I gonna plant this on Yaj? And where did she get these gadgets anyway? Did she belong to a paper that did sting operations on celebrities?

'Why don't they make it more sensibly shaped?'

'Like what?'

'Like…like a pack of cigarettes, for instance.'

'And what if our friend decides to light one?'

'Yeah…we'd get caught, wouldn't we?'

'Smart boy!'

I thought I detected a hint of sarcasm, but I let it be.

It was not as if I could just saunter into Yaj's room and leave the contraption lying around. Admittedly, we were on friendlier terms these days than we had been at the start of the series. But I wasn't exactly sure that those terms included a tolerant attitude towards my planting a recorder disguised as a lipstick, or any other piece of feminine accessory, in his room. Plus, there was the minor point of retrieving the device after it had, hopefully, served its purpose. That, in my book, simply doubled the risk. If I didn't get caught planting it, I could still get caught trying to retrieve it.

A dull ache was beginning to assault the melon, a clear indication that the grey matter was being put to the test. I rubbed my forehead vigorously with my thumbs, but this failed to produce any results worth note.

My problems only got slightly more compounded when she handed me one more of that ghastly device to be tagged on to Roshan. I consoled myself with the thought that if I could figure out how to plant one, I could definitely work out how to plant another.

That night I walked up to Yaj's room after having made sure that he was not around. His roommate, Giri, was visibly surprised to see me, especially considering how meticulously I had avoided going anywhere near Yaj's room in any of the hotels we had stayed in so far in the series.

'Hi,' he said, 'did you miss a turn or something on the way to your room? It is the third one on the corridor to the left of the elevator.' I studied his expression to see if there was a hint of a smile or anything that would tell me he was pulling my leg. But I found no such signs. Our opening bat was nothing if not, the epitome of seriousness.

'No...I actually came to see you,' I lied through my teeth.

'Oh, sure...come in,' said the diminutive southpaw, moving away from the door to let me in.

As soon as I entered the room, I scanned the place for a potential spot to place the device. I could feel its uncomfortable presence in my pocket and wanted to get rid of it at the earliest. I was pleased to note the general messy state of the suite, especially of the room that Yaj clearly occupied as was evidenced by the presence of a framed mugshot of the man on the dressing table. The untidiness, I hypothesised, would increase the chances of the recording device going unnoticed.

Giri had momentarily disappeared from my side and I could hear him rummaging about in the kitchen. I saw my chance and darted across to Yaj's room. Scanning the dressing table quickly, I found a vase with a bunch of plastic flowers sticking out of it. I hurriedly pulled the bunch out, switched on the device the way Nisha had showed me, thrust it into the vase and shoved the flowers back in, all the while wondering why a five-star hotel chose to serve its patron plastic flowers. I had barely replaced the vase on the table when I felt a tap on my shoulder. I nearly jumped out of my skin.

'Here,' said Giri, extending a can of soft drink to me. 'What are you doing here, in Yaj's room?'

'Oh,' I said, 'Oh...' My brain fumbled frantically for a suitable excuse but came up with nothing.

'Come,' said Giri, 'let's go to the balcony. It has a great view of the Motera.'

We hung out at the balcony for some time and Giri filled me in on some details about the wicket at the Motera, but my mind was not on it. I was on the verge of a nervous breakdown, my super-tingled nerves refusing to settle down after my recent tryst with espionage.

After about fifteen minutes, I muttered some excuse about having to make a few calls and took leave of Giri.

'Hey, buddy,' he called after me, 'nice talking to you. Drop in whenever you can. I'm sure Yaj will like it too. He's been wanting to talk to you for some time now.'

'Sure,' I said and dashed around the corner to my suite.

It was only later when I was in the relatively safer confines of my room that a horrible thought wormed its way into my head—what if Giri told Yaj about my visit, prompting Yaj to suspect something fishy and search his room? What if he discovered the strange contraption from the vase?

I had a tough time sleeping that night. I simply had to speak to someone. I tried calling Nish, but she didn't answer the call.

After tossing and turning around for a good thirty minutes, I finally climbed out of bed, walked over to Vijay's room and knocked on the door. The door opened instantly, revealing a sight that was so unexpected that I took a double take. Vijay was standing there as entirely expected in his pajamas and as entirely unexpected in pads, gloves and helmet as well, wielding his mace-like bat.

For a few seconds, I stood staring at this spectacle. I even rubbed my eyes, wondering if that would make this vision disappear. It didn't.

'Are you...practicing?'

He grunted in response and stepped aside, still holding the door open. I took this as an invitation to step inside. Vijay continued to shadow-bat shots, with the by-now-famous pronounced lack of feet movement. I almost wanted to point it out to him, but the usually unflappable Vijay looked like a man that even Christopher Columbus would not dare to cross.

Finally, he became bored of the exercise. Or, perhaps, my presence in the room finally percolated into his brain, releasing it from its meditative state. Whatever be the reason, he put his bat down and turned to face me.

'My balance at the crease is all wrong,' he said, by way of explanation for his attire and behaviour. 'What is your problem? Why are you up so late?'

'Well…I was having trouble sleeping…I…'

'I can understand, my boy,' said Vijay in a patronising voice, putting an arm around my shoulder. 'I remember my debut series against Sri Lanka…I was nervous as hell…but once I got that first hundred, things really settled down. You just focus on your game, son, and everything will be fine.'

'It's not just that, Vijay….I mean, of course, I'm nervous about my game…I have never seen a crowd like the one at the Eden Gardens….but it is not really that…I don't know how to tell you this.'

Vijay looked at me and then nodded meaningfully. Drawing closer, he asked in a conspiratorial whisper, 'Women problems?'

'W-what?'

'Not able to bat on that wicket, eh? Bowling too many no-balls? Can't get your leg-before-the-wicket?' he smirked.

I looked at him uncomprehendingly for a second. Then the meaning of what he was saying dawned upon me.

'Blushing, eh? So that is the problem?' he continued to smirk.

'No,' I protested, 'I mean…heck, I don't know about that…

but that's not...'

'Oh, so you are a maiden in that matter?'

'Maiden? You surely mean...virgin...don't you?'

'Same thing...So, are you?'

'Vijay, that's not the issue. I'm having...woman trouble... yes...but not that kind. You see, my friend, Nisha, has been wanting to...'

He cut me mid-sentence. 'She is wanting to? Then what's the problem, son? Just go ahead.'

'Vijay, can you pull your mind off that one-track path it is on right now and focus on what I'm trying to say?'

He assumed a look of seriousness under that helmet, ending up looking even more ridiculous in the process. 'You have my full attention, son. Go ahead.'

Before his thoughts strayed again, I blurted out all that I had to say in a rush, 'Nisha is a journalist. She is here to investigate the possibility of some match-fixing going on in this series. She thinks Yaj or Roshan is involved. I planted a recording device in Yaj's room and I have no clue how to plant it in Roshan's room. I am burning with guilt and at the same time I'm worried as hell that this is the last...the last opportunity we have before the series ends to identify this Judas...yes, I said "Judas"...and don't stare at me like that...you are making me nervous. Yes...it is our last chance to identify this traitor, if he exists, and expose him...and you've got to help me.'

Vijay stood with his mouth hanging open under that ridiculous helmet, looking as clueless as he had all series against some superb bowling by the Pakistani pacemen. Then he sat down and stared gravely at me for a full minute. I wouldn't exactly swear to it under oath, if it ever came to that, but it did look like a full minute to me.

'Say something, Vijay,' I said, when it looked like he might continue staring at me gravely for another minute.

'You know what, Nick? I have been bothered by the same thoughts for some time now. I am not too sure about the Mohali game, but the Kotla one sure smelt fishy. I was a bloody fool to play that stupid shot against that offspinner of theirs and there has not been a minute since when I have not kicked myself. But the way the rest of the batting folded up after I left was unbelievable!'

'What do we do, Vijay?'

'We should walk up right now to Monty and Bill and tell them all.'

'You think that's the way to go, Vijay? I just don't know.'

Vijay had risen up and was hurriedly taking off his pads. Clearly, the man could not wait to get the captain and coach in on the whole thing. But what I had just said made him hesitate.

'Are you sure about this, son? You know you don't level such charges lightly, don't you? You are talking about Yaj and Roshan who have served the nation for over a decade now. This is a serious allegation. I hope you are aware of it.'

'I am, Vijay…but Nisha seems convinced.'

'She could be so wrong, Nick.'

'But what if she were right, Vijay? Yaj, in particular has been struggling, hasn't he?'

'But he played so well today!'

'I know,' I conceded, 'but, anyway, the investigation has commenced. Vijay, I need your help. I want this device planted in Roshan's room. Help me, buddy...'

'If what you are saying is true, and there is a traitor in the team, I'd be the first one to want him caught. Give me that thing,' he said, reaching out for the device I held in my hand. 'How does this work?'

'Thanks a million, Vijay. Here, let me show you,' I said, showing him how to switch it on.'

'For all our sakes, Nick, let us pray that Nisha is wrong. Ideally, I should be taking the matter to Monty and Bill, but something tells me that your friend is wrong. I can't imagine Yaj or Roshan being involved in something like this. So, we better have proof before we take it up with the authorities. For the moment, let us keep this thing to ourselves. Now go and get some sleep. We have a huge game coming up tomorrow...and if what you said is true and there is a Judas in our midst, we would have to produce something extra special to win tomorrow.'

23

A Fatal Mistake

'*H*ey,' said Giri, as Yaj walked into their suite that evening. 'Where have you been, all afternoon?'

'Just stepped out for a while.'

'You look...worried. Are you alright?'

'Yeah...yeah...I'm quite ok. Just a little drained after the game. Why do you ask?'

'Nothing...you just look pale. You wanna drink or something?'

'Yeah...that would be nice. Could you get me something out of the fridge?'

'Sure,' said Giri. 'Hey, that reminds me...your friend, Nick, had come here a while ago.'

Yaj, who had been on his way to his room, stopped in his tracks.

'The kid looked a little lost,' said Giri, handing a can of

beer to Yaj. 'Said he'd come to see me.'

'Oh...what did he want?'

'Not sure...he looked very fidgety. Must be nerves. You know how we were during our first series, right? I just spoke to him to ease his nerves down a bit. Nice kid...I gave him a coke...there...the can is still on the table in your room.'

'He...he was in my room?'

'Yeah...dunno when he went in. Must have been when I went to fetch his drink. The guy nearly jumped when I tapped him on the shoulder.'

'What was he doing in my room?'

'Hey...nothing much...why are you so upset about it? He must have just wandered in.'

'Yeah...I'm sure that's it...Giri. I need to get some sleep, ok? Why don't you just run along and have dinner? I had something to eat...so I'm gonna skip.'

Saying so, Yaj shut the door to his room. Giri stood there for a while, unsure what had gotten into the man. Why was he reacting so strangely?

Yaj stood with his back to the closed door for a while, surveying the room. Now...why had that bugger come into his room?

The room looked as messy as he had left it. Had he always been this messy, he wondered. Or was it the events of the last few days had left him messed up enough not to have noticed how things were totally falling apart around him?

His eyes fell upon the table, taking in the diary, the pen stand and the vase of cheap flowers. Something seemed to be out of place, but he couldn't lay a finger on it. Even as he contemplated what it was, his cell phone rang, making him jump. Reluctantly, he pulled the instrument out and stared at the display. This had to end...

24

The Ahmedabad Blockbuster

The Motera game was a sellout. It simply had to be, considering that it was an India-Pakistan encounter and that India was playing to stay alive in the series. Like the Kolkatans, the Ahmedabadis thronged the ground in vast seas of patriotic blue. Unlike in Chandigarh, the Pakistani fan following wasn't as conspicuous in this city of businessmen in western India.

In front of a deafening crowd, Rashid Khan won the toss in this do-or-die battle, and promptly chose to bat. Historically, the Motera wicket has been a batsman's paradise, so Khan's decision did not prompt the eyebrows of the pundits to go swimming about their foreheads.

Roshan began proceedings for us and promptly had the Pakistani openers hopping around. Perhaps that prompted them to attack me, when I took the second new ball from the other end. They succeeded a little initially, when Salim slammed me for a couple of fours in the second over.

I realized that my mind was not entirely in the game. After my chat with Vijay, I had repaired to my room, but sleep had evaded me for another hour. Even as I was walking back to the mark on top of my runup, my mind was bubbling over with disturbing thoughts. I constantly found myself critically observing what Yaj and Roshan were doing. Why had Roshan overstepped the crease on the third ball of his third over? Hadn't he done the same in the previous game too? A no-ball off the third ball of his third over? Was that like spot-fixing or something? Was Yaj focusing hard enough? That misfield in the previous over looked too made up to me. Yaj could have stopped that ball in his sleep.

The thoughts came thicker and faster than the barrage of short balls that the Pakistani legend Wahab Anwar had unleashed on our hapless top order in the previous match and I reeled under the sustained onslaught. Consequently, Monty took me off the attack after my third over. I had conceded twenty-one runs in that little spell and looked nowhere as effective as I had at Chandigarh and Kolkata.

I was heartened to see Vijay keeping a hawk's eye on the team as well.

Over the next thirty overs, the game seesawed with both teams fighting to gain the upper hand. With the fortieth over of the game approaching, I could stand it no longer. I ran up to Monty and said, 'Skipper, I feel so ready to bowl now. Just gimme another shot.'

Monty gave me a cold, hard stare instead. Then his lips curled in a smile and he nodded thoughtfully. 'Roshan,' he shouted, 'you can go back to long-on. Nick is gonna bowl this one.' He slammed the ball into my palm and said, 'Go get them, tiger.'

For all my bravado, I wasn't exactly feeling like a tiger. Chicken would have been a more apt description. I could see the Pakistani batsmen licking their lips in anticipation at the sight of me with the ball. However, having snatched the ball from under Roshan's nose, I knew that there was no backing out.

It was perhaps this thought that acted as the drive I had been looking for. Suddenly, all thoughts of Judas and black sheep and spies and moles vanished from my mind to be replaced by the kind of concentration that had helped me bowl that dream spell to Yaj at Bangalore in what seemed like a lifetime ago.

I bowled my heart out. Bill would later tell me that he had never seen anyone bowl faster. All I knew was that I bowled my heart out in a five-over spell. At the end of it, all the Pakistani batsmen were back in the hut and I had my first five-wicket haul in limited overs cricket.

Everybody gathered around me and clapped me on the back until all the bones in my body had been thoroughly rattled. Monty handed me the match ball and I proudly marched around the ground, displaying the prized trophy.

We had restricted the Pakistanis to just 261. A target of 262 was not monumental by any stretch of the imagination on a wicket that continued to be batsman-friendly. However, we had underestimated the extent of the bad form that plagued our top order.

To their credit, both Vijay and Giri hung on to their

wickets by the proverbial skins of their teeth. Wahab Anwar was breathing fire and stomping the ground like the fabled iron bull that guarded the gates of the Motera stadium. And Vijay's repeated flashing outside the off stump was like a red rag to this raging bovine.

For the second time in that series, Vijay was instrumental in getting Giri run out. After having called him for a sharp single, our man sleepwalked back to the non-striker's end, leaving his partner high and dry. While Giri walked back to the pavilion mouthing voluble and entirely wholesome and unprintable curses, Vijay hammered his de-helmeted head repeatedly with his bat.

Out walked Yaj, with the Vivian Richardesque swagger from the previous game firmly in place. But there the comparison with the Caribbean legend ended. The man who had decimated the Pakistani attack in Kolkata suddenly looked out of sorts and the uncertainty of the Delhi and Chandigarh fixtures slowly clawed its way into his game.

This game was uncannily being played out almost exactly as the one at Chandigarh. First, the Pakistani score was just one short of the score they had set us at Mohali. Secondly, Vijay and Giri were involved in a run out, as they had been in that game. And now our batting superstars were treating us to an encore of their mind-numbing duet. I could see Monty, Viraj and Rana fidgeting in frustration.

Finally, Adil Mirza, the offspinner got one to turn into Yaj, rather than away and trapped him in front. I couldn't be very sure of it, but I think I saw Rashid Khan admonish his bowler for having got Yaj out. The spectators roared their approval at this unexpected turn of events that ended the most sleep-inducing session of play in the entire series. One commentator recommended playing a tape of the session to patients suffering from insomnia. Another suggested playing it to chronically depressed patients just to show them that their lives could not be as depressing as this and therefore, by corollary, there was hope.

The uncanny resemblance to the Mohali game continued, with Viraj, Rana and Monty playing out-of-their-skin cameos and taking the score within striking distance of the target.

Through this mayhem, Vijay plodded on with the dogged determination of an ox pulling a wagon. My heart went out to the man and I partly felt responsible for his present state. Many times I admonished myself for burdening Vijay with my worries when what the man needed the most was to unburden his mind and play like the free spirit that he usually was.

When Roshan and then Shiv joined Vijay in the center, my batting debut became a real possibility and I started squirming in my seat. If the butterflies in my stomach before my debut match had been the size of bats, they were now the size of MiG-29 fighter jets.

And then Shiv holed out to the fielder in the deep and my time had come.

The last words I heard before I set out on mission impossible was my captain yelling 'Cow corner!' emphasising his words by swinging his arms like a baseball hitter. It was clear that Vijay was struggling to put bat on ball, but to his credit, the man was hanging in there even as wickets were falling all around him like the sets of a disaster movie in the climax scene.

The Pakistani fielders were patrolling the infield like a pack of wolves that had smelt blood. I took guard against their fastest bowler Wahab Anwar, who looked like he ate batsmen for breakfast every day. As the towering Pathan thundered down the runway, I heard someone in the slips say, 'Hey kid, your pajamas are undone.' I stupidly gazed down for a fleeting second, before realizing I had been taken for a big ride. As I looked up, I saw the ball kicking off the pitch and played a shot out of pure self-preservation. I felt the ball hit the shoulder of the bat. Unsure where the ball had landed, I responded to Vijay's call, ran blind and just made it to the non-striker's end as the ball crashed into the wickets. I had my first run in international cricket off the first ball I faced! I had also nearly lost my wicket to the first ball I faced.

As I stood behind the popping crease at the non-striker's end, I chided myself for nearly falling prey to sledging. Some smartass in the slips had caused me to lose my focus and nearly earned me a golden duck on debut and cost us the game and the series. I swore to shut out the yapping that was bound to happen whenever I was batting and within audible range of the slips and close-in fielders.

Vijay took a mighty swing at the last ball of the forty-seventh and missed. That meant I would face the first ball of the forty-eighth over.

The situation was grim. We needed thirty-six off eighteen balls, with just one wicket in hand. The odds were clearly loaded in favour of the fielding team. After my calisthenics off the previous ball, it was only natural that the Pakistani captain would want me surrounded and that at least one 'perfume ball' was coming my way. The perfume ball is another of cricket's colourful expressions, used to describe a ball that went so close to the batsman's nose that he would be able to smell the 'perfume' of the leather. As expected, the field closed in when I took guard to take the first ball of the forty-eighth over.

I surveyed the field quickly and saw that the outfield was nearly unguarded. There was just one fielder on the offside outside the circle. Suddenly, as if by magic, the cobwebs enveloping my brain cleared and I felt a strange light illuminating my thoughts. If I was guessing it right, this ball was going to be a nasty short one on the off stump. If I picked it early, I realized I had a great chance to play it over the infield on the offside and get some runs.

As predicted, Syed Rehman, running in from the pavilion end, bowled a short one a bit wide outside the off stump. I saw my opportunity, swung the good piece of willow in my hand and made sound contact. The ball flew over the infield and raced away to the fence for a boundary. My first four! The crowd that had been silenced by the collapse of our middle order suddenly erupted. I knew it wasn't exactly a copy book shot, but as on other occasions that day, I wasn't complaining.

As I settled into my stance for the next ball, many thoughts invaded my head. Would he serve up another one outside off stump? Something told me that he would not. Instead, he would most probably over-compensate and pitch one at my toes. I made up my mind to swing at this one as well. The fact that the required run rate was running at the rate of knots made my choice easier. I simply had to go for it!

Rehman did exactly as I thought. He fired one in on the

leg stump. Even as he was at the point of releasing the ball, I took two steps backward, creating room to swing my arms. The ball landed right under the bat as it descended in a wide arc. I heard the impact, but did not feel it, because the timing was perfect...I guess. I watched as the ball disappeared into the crowd over long on. Six, over the cow corner!

Suddenly, I was beginning to enjoy this game. I closed my eyes and pictured the next ball and knew that it would arrive with the sole intention of knocking my head off my shoulders. I would have to duck or lose my head. I looked around casually and saw the fielder who had been at third man move over to fine leg, further confirming my theory. This one was definitely going to be short and bowled at middle and leg.

A very agitated Rehman thundered in to bowl the third ball of the over. Again, my prediction was spot on. He banged the ball into the pitch, causing it to rise a little over shoulder level. Having anticipated this, I had backed off a couple of feet away from the leg stump and had enough room to guide the ball over the slips. The extra pace of the bowler took the ball over the recently vacated third man region for another six! I realized that the risk had paid off, but only just.

Twenty-two runs were now needed off fifteen balls. Very achievable, but then all the Pakistanis needed was one good ball to end this run. As I prepared to face the next ball, I realized I had no clue what it would be. As Rehman released the ball, I made up my mind and charged down the pitch to meet it. This time I got an inside edge that missed the stumps and the gloves of the diving keeper and raced away to the fine leg boundary for four more. I had survived the first three balls because I had managed to get into the head of the bowler. The fourth one had been sheer luck. One inch to the right and the match would have been over. I wasn't sure when my luck would run out and decided I needed to be more careful.

Therefore, I defended the next ball and took a single off the sixth. It spoke volumes about the state of mind Vijay was in when he consented to take a single off the last ball, thereby letting me take strike against Anwar in the next over.

We now needed seventeen to win off twelve balls. The field was now much more spread out, thanks to the big hits in the previous over. I thought this was a defensive move. By cutting down on the options of getting one of us out, they were merely increasing our chances of pulling off an upset.

The first ball was a scorching toe crusher that I just managed to keep out. Thanks to the gaps now available in the infield, I was able to call Vijay through for a single. Vijay attempted to slam the next ball through cover, but mistimed it. We ran the first one real quick, but I could see that my partner was struggling and would never make the second, so I sent him back.

I had to block two balls from the champion bowler because they were simply unplayable. I realized that I was unable to out-think Anwar as I had Rehman. Even as I was thinking that this man was of a different cut, he proved he was not without faults by bowling a juicy half-volley. I swung hard, sending the ball flying over the head of the bowler, neatly bisecting the fielders at long on and long off, for another boundary. Eleven needed off seven balls.

With the last ball of the over coming up and a tail-ender

on strike, most captains would have no hesitation in spreading the field and allowing the single so that the tail-ender, and by definition the weaker batsman, would be on strike for the first ball of the new over.

But I could see that Rashid Khan was not sure if that was what he wanted to do. Although I was officially the tail-ender, I had shown some decent form in the previous couple of overs and it was Vijay who was behaving like the mug with the bat. In the end, utterly unsure as to whom he wanted on strike, Rashid Khan ended up giving us a field that was an in-between kind of affair. It neither protected the boundary entirely, nor did it prevent the single. And to make matters worse, Anwar bowled another half-volley, which I gladly tonked through midwicket and we ran three.

We now needed just eight off the last over and I was on strike. Khan boldly tossed the ball to Rehman, in spite of the atrocious previous over he had bowled. The field was defensive, with four men patrolling the boundary and even the in-fielders stationed at the very edge of the inner circle. I had plenty of opportunities to take the single. But something told me not to...that Vijay would not be able to take us across the finishing line.

Unlike at the start of the previous over, when he had been bristling with confidence, Rehman did not thunder in. Instead, he wobbled in unsteadily like my old Lambretta and delivered an innocuous slower ball that even my mom could have swatted with a broomstick. Being equipped with a piece of wood that was significantly better than a broomstick, I danced down the wickets and slammed him over his head. The ball rose high into the Ahmedabad sky, described a neat little parabola and disappeared into the stands over the sight screen.

The crowd went ballistic. Gujarati versions of the Mexican wave began doing the rounds of the stadium to the tunes of *garba* numbers. That, to my mind, was the decisive blow. With just two runs needed off five balls, the game was well and truly in our hands. There was one anxious moment, though, when the bowler bowled a beauty that nearly took the edge of my bat off the next ball. The bowler and the fielders threw their hands up and tossed their heads back in agony. Even Vijay looked like he had escaped a cardiac arrest by the narrowest of margins. With a concerned look, he walked over to me and patted my shoulders a couple of times to calm me down.

Rashid Khan seemed to have woken up to the situation finally and he set a test match-worthy field. The infielders closed in like a pack of wolves, desperation writ large in their eyes as they looked to get that one wicket to seal the series.

But it was not to be. That one delivery which had nearly kissed the varnish of my bat in the previous ball happened to be the only bright moment in an otherwise dark evening for Rehman. The next ball seemed to slip out of his hands down the leg side and all I had to do was to ensure I got some wood on it to send it on its way to the fine leg boundary and seal an improbable win for India.

The deafening roar was the loudest I had ever heard and it possibly drowned out all other sounds in the state of Gujarat for the next minute or so. It certainly drowned out the screams and whoops of joy of my teammates as they rushed in a drove onto the field, engulfing Vijay and me in a swarm of blue.

As we were carried around the stadium, I looked at Vijay. The man had battled his own bad form and played an entirely out-of-character innings for all of fifty overs just to ensure that we were home and dry. It was the most painstaking knock of his career. To me, it was also the most heroic knock I had ever seen.

It was not very surprising that I won the man of the match award. After all, I had taken five wickets and then scored an unbeaten forty off just fifteen balls. It had surely been the most impactful performance of the day from either side. Although I was not surprised, I was completely over the moon with joy. For one, Mom and Dad had made it to the stadium for the first time in the series, having entirely missed my debut game and the one in Kolkata. Secondly, when I saw established stalwarts like Yaj and Vijay struggling, I realized that success was a fickle-minded companion at the best of times and, therefore, it was vitally important to savour it on the occasions that it chose to smile upon you.

The presence of a certain Miss Nisha was also a major factor in the elation I felt. I thought of her as I walked to the podium to collect my prize. Inevitably, thoughts of Mission Inside Edge and the unpleasant tasks that awaited my attention also clouded the mind. But only momentarily. I realized that I was just a young bloke who deserved to enjoy the few moments of glory while they lasted. Let me take in the bouquets while they come, I reasoned. The brickbats would follow as surely as night followed day. But I would cross that bridge when I came to it. For now, my motto was, 'Why so serious?'

25

Partners in Crime

$\mathcal{V}$ijay and I snuck out of the bar about thirty minutes after the celebrations had begun and most of our colleagues were sufficiently drunk not to notice our absence. I found it especially difficult, since I was the centre of attention that evening and had been drenched in a copious amount of champagne. It had taken a supreme amount of self-control to merely pretend to sip the one glass that Monty had thrust in my hand, even as the liquid flowed freely everywhere. I was secretly glad that Mom and Dad had chosen to give the party a miss. Mom would surely have had a nervous breakdown seeing her only son swimming about in all that alcohol.

At the other end of the room, Vijay was also doing his best to maintain a safe distance from the champagne. Considering that he was a person who believed in preserving his innards in alcohol, this came as a supreme sacrifice. Catching my eye, my partner-in-crime nodded almost imperceptibly. It was time.

All suites in the hotel had access cards and Vijay had somehow managed to pilfer the cards to Yaj's and Roshan's rooms. Handing me the card to Yaj's room, he moved to the part of the floor where Roshan and Rana were put up.

I stood outside the door to Yaj's suite for a few seconds, suddenly hesitant to do what I had come to do. It felt uncomfortably like I was breaking in or something. I considered why I was feeling like that, for a minute, and came to the conclusion that it could only be because that was exactly what I was doing. I was indeed breaking in. Having worked out that logic, I put the thought out of my mind and swiped the card. An electronic beep told me that the lock had released. I pushed the door open and stepped inside.

I walked past Giri's room to Yaj's. It was as messy as the last time I had been there. I quickly moved to the dressing table and plucked the flowers out of the vase. The recording device was still there. Placing it on the table, I quickly put the flowers back in the vase and turned to leave, when...

'What are you doing here?'

My heart had nearly stopped and I clutched at the table to prevent from collapsing altogether.

Giri walked into the room, eyeing me suspiciously. 'Don't tell me you came to meet me. You saw me down at the bar with the rest of the boys. You obviously didn't come to meet Yaj, either. So, tell me, why are you here?'

'I...I...'

'I'll tell you, Giri,' said Vijay, materialising out of nowhere. Turning to me, he said, 'No point hiding it now, Nick. The game is up.' Turning to Giri, he said, 'Giri, old friend, can you keep a secret?'

'Sure,' said Giri, sounding anything but sure.

'Nick is a cross-dresser.'

'What!' both Giri and I cried in unison.

'You don't believe me, Giri? Look at that thing he has in his hand,' said Vijay, pointing to the recording device I was holding. 'What does it look like to you?'

Giri screwed up his eyes, scrutinizing the device. 'Well, it looks like a...like a...'

'Tube of lipstick?' prompted Vijay, rather helpfully.

'Yes...I think.'

'Well, it is a tube of lipstick.'

This time, I actually staggered and almost fell. But then I quickly recovered. 'Well, Giri, you might want to check what Vijay has in his pocket,' I said, pointing to a telltale bulge in Vijay's shirt pocket.

Reluctantly, Vijay pulled out the device he had recovered from Roshan's suite.

Giri looked shocked. 'You...you guys...are queer?'

'Yes,' said Vijay and I, glaring at each other.

'Wow!...Wow!...I really don't know what to say!'

'You may want to sit down and digest the information,' offered Vijay, helpfully.

'Yes...I would like to sit down...wow!'

'Well...we should take our leave, then,' said Vijay, making for the door.

'Wait,' said Giri, like a man who had just laid a finger on something he had been trying to lay a finger upon for some time.'Wait...that does not explain why you guys are in my suite.'

'Well, Vijay...would you like to tell our good friend why we are in his suite?'

'Sure, Nick,' said Vijay, looking at me like one would at something particularly disgusting that had crawled out from under a rotting log of wood. 'You see, Giri, Nick and I were particularly bored of trying our queerness in our own suite. We were just not getting the...how do you put it...right feeling. We thought a change of ambience would get us into the proper mood.'

My jaw dropped. With a resigned shake of my head, I followed Vijay out of the suite, leaving a thunderstruck Giri in our wake.

26

Judas Speaks

*T*he final game of the series, the decider, was to be played in my hometown, Bangalore. The day after the Ahmedabad game, we landed at the Bangalore International Airport. All the Malleswaram Mavericks had gathered at the airport, along with a huge throng of Team India fans, to receive us. It was very unnerving and funny to see people that I had grown up with rooting for me. It was decidedly good, but it was also unnerving, all the same.

On the eve of the match, Nisha, Vijay and I gathered in her room.

With a very serious air entirely becoming the situation, Nisha dismantled the device to recover the recording unit. It was about the size of a shirt button, only a few millimeters thicker. This she proceeded to insert into a slot in another device, which was connected to her laptop.

'Did you have trouble retrieving it?' she asked, as she waited for the audio file to download.

'I don't wanna talk about it, Nish...really.'

'What about you, Vijay?'

'I'd rather not talk about it, too.'

She looked at us with an amused air, trying to guess what might have happened that was obviously causing us quite a bit of embarrassment. A ping sound from her laptop announced that the file had been downloaded and she turned her attention to it. 'Literally saved by the bell,' I thought.

'Here we go, Nick. This might just tell us if we are chasing the right man, after all,' she said, trying to infuse some drama into the situation.

She double-clicked the icon on the screen and the three of us huddled together in anticipation. Presently, a voice we recognized as Yaj's floated in. He was talking to Giri. We sat through a couple of minutes of conversation that was entirely meaningless to the investigation. Then, the distinct sound of a cell phone ringing was heard and our ears perked up as Yaj answered the call.

'*Tell me.*' His voice was curt, as if this was a call he wasn't exactly looking forward to.

'*You wanna meet me! Why?*'

'*Look, it isn't exactly easy for me to just walk out of our hotel and meet you at some godforsaken place.*'

He listened to what the person at the other end had to say.

'*Why do you wanna meet? You know it's risky. I can't be seen about in public with you! I have done all that you ever asked me to. Why meet?*' He was almost pleading.

A whole minute followed, when Yaj was listening again. Even through the recording, one could cut the tension with a knife.

'*I will meet you…this once…just this once…because if I don't you'll screw up my life! I will do as you say because with that one mistake, I have sold my soul to the devil,*' he screamed.

'See,' Nisha whispered, 'I told you he was being blackmailed.'

'Nisha,' Vijay whispered right back, 'you don't have to whisper. He can't hear us through the recording.'

We burst out laughing. Trust Vijay to break the tension.

'Sh…sh…sh,' said Nish, 'We missed what he just said. Let me rewind a little.'

'*Where? Golden Sand? My my…your standards have improved, I must say! No more meeting in seedy restaurants?*'

'*Ok…I will be there at 8. I hope to God that this is the last time we meet.*'

There was the sound of the phone audio being abruptly killed. This was followed by a few minutes of audio that was not clear. Presumably, Yaj was preparing to go meet the person he had just spoken to. Then there was the sound of a door slamming shut, followed by silence.

'Well,' said Nisha after allowing a decent amount of time for us to get our bearings, 'what do you make of it?'

'I don't know, Nisha,' said Vijay, at length. 'I have known this guy over a decade. I have played with him and admired the passion he always brought to the game. It is heartbreaking to see him like this. Trust me, he would not do something like this for money. That dog he was talking to definitely has something on him. Didn't you hear him say that he had sold his soul to the devil?'

'That may be true, Vijay, but that doesn't let him off the hook. He has committed a crime against you, the team and the country.'

I thought she was being jingoistic. I also thought she was jumping the gun. After all, we only had a one-sided conversation in the name of evidence.

Vijay clearly looked ruffled and I sympathized with him. I could understand his dilemma. After all, how do you doubt a man who has been like a brother for over a decade and has stood with you though thick and thin?

'All said and done, I won't have peace until I dig deeper into this matter,' said Vijay. 'I must absolutely find out if Yaj is involved with match fixers. Nick, I know this place he was referring to in the tape. We should leave now,' he said, looking at his watch. 'We have about ten minutes to get to the hotel and catch him red-handed. I hope to God that we are mistaken and Yaj is clean.'

'That's right, Nick. Why don't you and Vijay go to this hotel and see who Yaj is meeting? I will quickly tidy up things here,' she said, indicating the other transmitter lying on the bed. 'If Yaj is not our man, then we better have something to carry on our investigation.'

'Meet me outside the hotel, Nick. I don't want people, especially Bill, to see both of us leaving together. I will call a cab to pick us up in the meanwhile. Let's not take the hotel cab. If Yaj sees one from the hotel's fleet, he'll know he's being followed.'

Five minutes later, Vijay and I took a cab into the quiet

late evening. We drove past the parks and high-rises of the city before crossing into the suburbs.

'This hotel seems to be quite out of the way,' I remarked, after our cab had traveled a good fifteen minutes. Although I was the local boy, I had never heard of this hotel.

'Logical, isn't it? A celebrity, like Yaj, would not care to be seen with shady characters in the heart of a city where he is likely to be recognized. For meetings of this kind, a secluded place is best.'

I saw the point and was glad to have the calm, even-minded Vijay by my side on this nerve-jangling journey.

Soon, we were driving along Banerghatta Road. Five minutes after we passed Hulimau Gate, the cab took a left off the main road and entered a heavily wooded region.

'Are you sure we are going the right way, Vijay?'

'I...guess so...though this part of town looks unfamiliar to me,' he replied. Gently tapping the cabbie on the shoulder, he asked, 'Are you sure this is the way to the Golden Sand hotel?'

'Yes, sir,' replied the cabbie, in heavily accented Hindi. 'We take this road through the woods and then meet an interstate on the other side.'

The road grew narrower and disappeared into little more than a mud track. There were no streetlights and the rustic nature of the path was illuminated in equal measure by the powerful headlamps of the car and the severe jolts we were subjected to in the passenger seat.

The car drew to a halt at the doors of what looked like a log cabin, the kind you read about in stories from the Wild West. The dim light leaking out from a lone window indicated that the cabin was occupied.

The driver slid out of his seat and came over to the window to my right. I stared, mesmerized, down the barrel of a gun he held in his right hand. He opened the door, motioning me to step out. 'Come out with your hands behind your head,' he said, for the benefit of Vijay, 'and no smart stuff or I'll blow his brains off.'

'Do as he says, Nick,' said Vijay, quite unnecessarily, as he stepped out of the car in the manner prescribed by our abductor. I had no intention of doing anything other than what was being suggested.

Two other burly characters stepped out of the cabin and took up positions behind us, presumably to prevent us from dashing off into the woods. To me, this was an unnecessary precaution. I, for one, had no intention of doing anything even remotely stupid and Vijay's demeanour did not suggest anything to the contrary either.

We were paraded into the cabin and tied securely to two chairs, back-to-back. This didn't look like your regular mugging and showed a distinct leaning towards kidnapping. Not that it made me feel any better. I was still struggling to come to grips with the way things were rapidly spiraling out of control.

The men who had abducted us stepped outside the cabin. Clearly, the driver of the cab was the leader of the gang.

I turned to Vijay. But before I could say a word, he began, 'Don't even bother asking me what this is all about, Nick, because I have absolutely no idea. I just wish I had not let you and that girlfriend of yours talk me into this nonsense. Here I am already battling problems of my own and you have gone and dragged me into this! Now the best you can do is to shut up, stop asking me questions and let me think how I can get us out of this mess.'

I was a bit taken aback by the assault and opened and closed my mouth a couple of times, like a fish out of water, but could not think of anything to say. All hopes of escape were useless. Nisha would probably call the cops if we didn't turn up in the next two hours or so, but all she would be able to tell them would be that we were at hotel Golden Sand. The 'evidence' she had against Yaj would not stand in a court of law because it was a one-sided conversation that could have meant just about anything. Our only hope was that she had uncovered something from the device we had planted on our other suspect. Even if something did turn up there, it still did not help us overcome our present predicament. For all practical purposes, Vijay and I were dead.

Before tying us up, the kidnappers had taken away our wallets and my cell phone. These articles were lying on a table, agonisingly out of reach. While Vijay retired to his private world of thoughts, I tried to work out how to lay my hands on the phone.

The fact that my hands were tied up behind me made it even more difficult to wrench them free. But I tried all the same, feeling the rope cut into my wrists. And then I felt it... something solid, roughly rectangular in shape. It was in Vijay's jacket pocket.

Carefully, I maneuvered my hand into the pocket and extracted the thing. It felt like...I couldn't believe it...it felt like a cell phone! They had overlooked Vijay's cell phone!

A sense of exhilaration spread through my body, like a ray of hope had been kindled somewhere.

'Vijay?'

'Shut up!'

'Listen to me, Vijay,' I hissed.

'What?'

Before I could speak, the door flung open and the three men walked in. I quickly cupped the phone in my palm, trying my best to hide it, thankful for its small size.

'Feed our guests,' said the leader, indicating the two trays of food his goons had brought in.

'Why have you brought us here?' I asked.

'Ah! Wouldn't you like to know? Well, you see, your girlfriend has been right all along. There is indeed a stooge of mine in your team...and yes...he has been fixing games for me.'

Suddenly, a thought occurred to me. I wanted this conversation transmitted. I knew I would be unable to dial Nisha's number with my hands tied up the way they were. But I had to absolutely make sure that the conversation was transmitted. How could I do it? Yes...the phone...But if I dialed, would the person I called pick it? Would the conversation be audible enough? There was no way of knowing that. But what chance did I have. With that thought in mind, I pressed a key twice, redialing the number that was last dialed from the phone.

'He screwed up the first two games of the series and almost did your team in the third...'

Suddenly, a cell phone went off in the room, startling all of us and cutting the man mid-sentence. I frantically cut the call I was making even as the man fumbled for his phone in his jacket pocket. With a shock, I realized that his phone had stopped ringing the moment I cut the call. Could it be...?

'As I was saying...'

This time I did not cut the call. The phone blared away even as he pulled it out of his pocket and stared hard at the screen. Then, slowly, he looked at Vijay in disbelief.

27

A Shocking Discovery

*N*isha waited a few minutes after Nick left the hotel room. Then, she picked up her phone and dialed a number.

'Yes…they have just left…Nick is meeting Vijay outside the gate…yes…a cab…outside the gate.'

She snapped the phone shut and looked at the recording devices on the table. She picked up the one that had been planted in Roshan's room. She plugged the device to her laptop and started downloading the file, when she noticed that the window playing the recording from Yaj's room was still open. She activated the window with the intention of listening to the audio again.

She was about to hit the rewind button when her eyes fell upon the progress bar. Apparently, they had only heard about eighty per cent of the recording. Curious, she hit the play button.

Some strange rustling sounds filled the air. There was also the sound of someone hurriedly pushing away a chair and then the sound of a door opening and closing. That was possibly Nick retrieving the device, she thought. In his hurry to get away, the idiot had forgotten to switch it off.

'*What are you doing here?*' Nisha couldn't exactly place the voice. She hadn't heard it before.

'*Don't tell me you came to meet me. You saw me down at the bar with the rest of the boys. You obviously didn't come to meet Yaj, either. So, tell me, why are you here?*'

'*I...I...*' That was obviously Nick. The bloody fool had been caught retrieving the device!

'*I'll tell you, Giri. No point hiding it now, Nick. The game is up. Giri, old friend, can you keep a secret?*'

Giri! And wasn't that Vijay?

'*Sure.*'

'*Nick is a cross-dresser.*'

'*What!*'

Nisha's hand flew to her mouth as she tried to suppress a giggle. '*What!*'

'*You don't believe me, Giri? Look at that thing he has in his hand. What does it look like to you?*'

'*Well, it looks like a...like a...*'

'*Tube of lipstick?*' Nisha marveled at Vijay's ingenuity.

'*Yes...I think.*'

'*Well, it is a tube of lipstick.*'

'*Well, Giri, you might want to check what Vijay has in his pocket.*'

'*You...you guys...are queer?*'

'Yes.' By now, Nisha was laughing very hard.

'Wow!...Wow!...I really don't know what to say!'

'You may want to sit down and digest the information.'

'Yes...I would like to sit down...wow!'

'Well...we should take our leave, then.'

'Wait...Wait...that does not explain why you guys are in my suite.'

'Well, Vijay...would you like to tell our good friend why we are in his suite?'

'Sure, Nick...You see, Giri, Nick and I were particularly bored of trying our queerness in our own suite. We were just not getting the...how do you put it...right feeling. We thought a change of ambience would get us into the proper mood.'

Nisha was now literally rolling on the floor, laughing her guts out. No wonder Nick and Vijay were so reluctant to talk about their adventures while retrieving the devices. 'Cross dressers!' 'Proper mood!'...oh boy!

The recording played on...More sounds...Nick walking down the corridor and entering his room. Then, relative silence for a few seconds, followed by the sound of the door closing.

She was about to shut the window down, when the sound of a very garish ringtone filled the air. She had heard that tone before, but could not remember where.

'Noor?' a very familiar voice answered the call.

'Noor, I was waiting for you to call...listen, there is trouble... big trouble...yes, the boy and, more importantly, his girlfriend are on to the case like a pair of hounds...No...I don't think they suspect me yet...but it is only a matter of time...what do you want me to do?....What?...Are you insane?...Surely you are *joking! What do you mean kidnap?'*

There was a moment of silence as the man listened on the phone.

'Is there no other way?' his voice sounded resigned.

'Very well...I will bring him to you...see to it that no harm comes to him...he is just a boy. Give me your word that you'll release him as soon as it is safe to.'

Nisha listened to the conversation with increasing horror. She had remembered where she had heard the ringtone. The man's voice was also unmistakable. Nick was in real danger.

She picked up her phone and dialed a number.

28

A Cat Out of the Bag

'So, it was you!' I said, my voice drained of all emotion.

'What are you talking about, man?'

'Here, you might want your phone back.' I flicked the phone, hoping it would land on Vijay's lap. It did.

'You…you called…from this phone?…Oh, shit! Oh, bloody shit!' The horror of the whole situation seemed to have dawned upon Vijay, as was evidenced in his voice.

'Apparently, he did,' said our captor, cutting in. 'And so there is no further need to continue this pretence or to keep you tied-up. The cat is out of the bag.'

'I can explain, Nick…I…I really can.'

'Shut your trap, you lousy son-of-a…'

'Nick…I really can…gimme a chance.'

'You son-of-a-bitch! So that night when I caught you screaming at someone in the loo, you were actually talking to this...this son-of-a-bitch, right?'

'Hey, hey, hey...you two birds...cut down your lover's spat.'

'Why did you do it, Vijay? And to think that I walked up to you to help me with the investigation!'

'He made me do it, Nick.'

'Oh, good! Confession time, eh? Go ahead, unburden your guilt. Then I can shoot him and you can mop his brains off the floor.' Noor brandished the gun.

'What! Shoot me!'

'What? Noor...you gave me your word...you can't harm him. Put that gun away!'

'You kidding me, man? After he has discovered our secret, you expect me to let him live?'

'You can't be serious!' both of us said at once.

In reply, Noor released the safety catch of his weapon.

29

A Game of Shadows

About two minutes after Vijay and Nick's cab left the highway and turned into the woods, a black sedan did the same. The car halted about fifty metres from the cabin. Inspector Chinnappa stepped out, followed by a colleague. Both of them pulled out service revolvers from their coats and noiselessly crept towards the cottage.

A dense growth of bushes surrounded the log cabin, some of them tall and thick enough to hide behind. The two cops concealed themselves behind the bushes and observed the happenings outside the cabin.

The cab in which Nick and Vijay had travelled from the hotel was parked outside the cabin. The driver, a well-built fellow with a thick stubble stepped out. Even in the dim moonlight, the inspector could see how closely the man resembled the sketch the software had produced based on the descriptions provided by the bookie and his girlfriend.

The driver stood near the door, brandishing what looked like a semi-automatic. The said firearm was pointed at the occupants of the car. Two men popped out of the cabin and took positions behind the car, presumably to prevent the occupants from attempting an escape. Moments later, Nick emerged from the car, with his hands held above his head. Vijay followed, and the two captives were muscled into the cabin.

The cops exchanged glances, nodded and crept closer to the cabin.

30

On the Proverbial Jaw

It's true what people say. With death just a trigger-pull away, a synopsis of your life does indeed run through your mind and all the moments you have lived to regret flash before the inner eye. In my case, it was a singularly beautiful picture of Nisha that projected itself. I dearly wished I had mustered the courage to express how I felt about her when I had the opportunity. Too late for that now!

Bang!

Had I kicked the bucket? Had I handed in my dinner pail? Had my appointment with the Grim Reaper finally come? In other words, was I dead? If I was, I wasn't much too worse for it. For one, I hadn't felt any pain and that in itself must count for something.

Three more bangs followed, each of a much higher acoustic level than the first.

I opened my eyes and took in the following scene, though not necessarily in the described order. Vijay was rooted to a spot, staring into the distance, swaying ever so slightly. A vaguely familiar man, who looked like he could essay the role of King Kong without too much difficulty, was standing with a gun in his hand surveying his handiwork, which, apparently, had caused the unexpected and hurried departure of Noor and his fellow goons from the world of the living. That this arrangement had not been to their liking was evident from the outraged expressions on their faces.

And, Nisha was the current occupant of my lap. Perhaps I had died and gone to heaven, after all! She had her arms around my neck and buried in my chest was her head, the gentle bobbing of which seemed to suggest that she was sobbing.

'Oh, Nick...my baby...my sweet baby...'

I was just coming to my own self, which, admittedly was not a vast improvement on the dizzy state of a few seconds ago and was only just beginning to take stock of the situation. I certainly was not dead...and I was quite glad for the fact. Strangely, and in a manner that was almost entirely irrelevant to my current circumstances, I was also glad that Bonsai and the rest of my cronies from back home were not around to witness the overall mushiness of the setting and the terms of endearment that were floating around. I'd never have heard the end of it. But, being the sort of guy that did not let trivial matters, such as the opinions of friends, come in the way of enjoying the unexpected pleasures that life did occasionally throw into one's lap...quite literally...I decided to do the right thing and go with the flow. Since no one had bothered to untie me, I limited myself to putting my head on hers, in a way I hoped was comforting.

'If you two love birds are done, could we all just dash along?' I think it was the guttural nature of the voice in which the words were uttered that brought me to my senses. In that state, my mind took in the scene again…and this time it registered the horror.

'C'mon darling…let's go.' I didn't need a second invitation. The hunk, who I had now positively identified as Gaurav (yes, the same Gaurav who had roughed me up at Koshy's, a lifetime ago) pushed a still-stunned Vijay along.

We ran down a path to a car parked in the bushes. Before hopping into the car, Gaurav dashed back into the cabin. Two minutes later, he returned, took the wheel and drove down a rugged path that opened out into the highway. I sat in the backseat, snuggled up with Nisha. Vijay sat slumped in front, showing no inclination to snuggle up with Gaurav. In fact, the man hadn't spoken a word since our rescue.

Some of the numbness that had enveloped my brain, and therefore protected it from much of the shock, was beginning to wear off. With increased realization came questions, far greater in number than my processor was accustomed to handle. As noble as Gaurav's intentions were, and make no mistake I'd be eternally grateful to the man for saving my life, his actions begged answers to some questions as to why there were a few killings involved. Then there was also the question of how he and Nisha had managed to show up just in time to save our miserable asses.

Nisha was beginning to show signs of recovering, in

that her head had progressed gradually from my chest to my shoulder. Also, her sobs had lost their original sense of urgency and were going about their business in a more relaxed sort of manner.

'Nish,' I asked, 'What's going on?'

She sat up and took a deep breath to compose herself. Something told me that I would need to brace myself for what she was going to say.

'Nick, I've not been entirely honest with you.'

The last time she had said that, we'd launched Mission Inside Edge. I wasn't sure the system was in any state to cope up with anything of that magnitude, yet.

'Oh...Ok...what do you mean?'

'I'm not a journalist.'

That was not too bad. Though it did qualify technically as being dishonest, it was not the sort of thing that shook relations to their very foundations. I must admit to a mild sense of relief carousing through my veins and the subconscious un-bracing of the self by a notch or two.

'I'm a cop.'

'W-what?' I stammered, instantly regretting the rather hasty un-bracing as a consequence of which my wretched soul had taken the full impact of this revelation on the proverbial jaw.

She pulled out an ID card. This one identified her as Inspector Nisha Chinnappa of the Karnataka State Police, the Government of India.

Yet again, I demonstrated how one is entirely capable of staggering even while seated on a plush seat, if one really put one's mind to it.

'I'll explain everything, Nick. Let us get to the hotel first. I'm sure Vijay has a lot to explain as well.'

The man continued to sit like a stone.

31

Confessions

$\mathcal{W}$e made it to the hotel in the wee hours of the morning. Fortunately, our absence had gone unnoticed and we were able to make it to our room quietly.

Nisha had composed herself superbly by now and once again looked like the woman in control. I watched her sitting pensively on the armchair. The fact that she was an officer of the law had not fully sunk in yet.

Vijay, who we had eased into the other armchair, suddenly threw his head back and let out a sigh. As signs go, this wasn't exactly a sign of revival but was a definite improvement from the stone statue he had been a second before.

I leapt from the bed to reach out to him. But before I could move even one foot, an icy cold voice cut through the room. 'Vijay, so would you like to tell us what was going on?'

A tear welled up in Vijay's right eye and streamed down his

cheek. A moment later a second stream followed from his left.

'Vijay, you must tell us. What happened was a serious crime. If you confide in us, we might be able to get you off the hook. I don't need to tell you what would happen if the people get a whiff of this.'

Vijay's throat pulsated once as he gently swallowed a lump.

'I don't know wh... where to begin.'

'How about at the beginning?' cut in Gaurav. 'Where did you meet this Noor?'

'At Bangalore...before the first camp.'

'Go on.'

'He called me and asked me to meet him.'

'Why?'

'He...he said he had something...to sh...show me.'

'What?'

'Please don't ask me...please.'

Gaurav was about to say something, when Nisha held up her hand. 'What did Noor ask you to do, Vijay?' she asked.

Vijay let out another sigh.

'You have to tell us, Vijay. That's the only way we could do something to help you. You've got to trust us.'

'Come on, buddy,' I prompted. I could see that the man was struggling within and my heart went out to him. I had grown to like this man in the little time that I had known him.

'He...he asked me to...tank games.'

'Did you?'

Vijay swallowed once more. The tears were now cascading down in steady rivulets.

'Answer me, Vijay...did you fix games in this series?' Her

voice was surprisingly gentle. Somewhere, perhaps, she felt his pain, too.

'Yes,' his voice was a hoarse whisper.

Deep inside, I already knew the answer, but it was still a shock to hear the man say it. Until that moment, I had nursed the hope that we were on a wild goose chase and match-fixing did not exist. With Vijay's admission, my hopes came crashing down. We had found our Judas.

'Was there anyone else involved?'

'Noor wanted me to g…get another guy involved. That new physio from New Zealand. He..he even got the guy's Indian girlfriend pulled in. But I never got a chance to talk to the man. So no one else involved.'

I rose from the bed and walked up to Vijay, brushing aside a restraining arm that Nisha stuck out. Nothing would have stopped me from looking my hero in the eye and demanding an answer to the questions that were burning in my heart. 'Why, Vijay? Why did you betray us?'

For the first time during the confession, Vijay opened his eyes and looked at me. 'I had to, Nick…I had no choice.'

'You had no choice? Other than to betray your brothers?'

'Nick, don't.'

'Don't stop me, Nish. I want to know how the man that I have looked up to for as long as I can remember had the heart to sell us to the devil. Tell me Vijay…what did he offer you? Money? How much money, Vijay? What did he offer you that you didn't have already?'

'Nick…I…'

'Gaurav?' said Nisha.

Gaurav nodded, pulled out an envelope from his pocket and handed it to Nisha.

'Perhaps this will tell you, Nick,' she said, handing the packet to me.

'Oh God,' an anguished cry escaped Vijay's lips and he threw up his hands to cover his face.

I opened the envelope and pulled out a photo. An instant later, I pushed it back with trembling hands. My shock was for Vijay and the realization of what he must have endured more than what I had seen in the photo. Of course, I hated him. That girl was no more than a child. What sort of sick man would do that to a child!

I flung the envelope away in disgust and walked back to the bed, where I sat holding my head in my hands.

'Gaurav found it when he hopped back into the cabin and did a quick search. The man, Noor, was carrying this in his windcheater.'

For a few seconds we all sat quietly, letting realization sink into our individual consciences.

'I...I had no choice, Nick. He had me by the balls... Noor threatened to release this all over the internet...to the media. He would have ruined my name...I have a family, Nick...It was too much of a price to pay for one moment of indiscretion.'

'Indiscretion? You son-of-a...you do that to a teen and call it indiscretion?' I had no idea why I was boiling. Somehow, I also realized that my anger was misdirected. No doubt, I was seething about his 'indiscretion', but what really had my goose was the fact that the miserable worm had sold us out to save his stinking skin.

'I am so sorry, Nick...you must...'

'Sorry my ass, you swine. Do you have any idea what you have done? While the rest of us sweated blood and ground our bones to the dust, you were busy sinking the ship! You lousy, stinking rat!' I was on a roll and would have done Ms Mallik, my drama teacher, proud.

Nisha was by my side. 'Nick, calm yourself,' she said, putting a reassuring arm around my waist. 'There was nothing Vijay could do.'

'Yes there was, Nish...there certainly was. He could have walked up to the team and poured his heart out. I have been a month with this bunch and I know how genuine these blokes are. Some of them may be bums, but they are so from-the-heart types. They'd have forgiven him.'

'The point is not that alone, Nick. There was always the threat of Noor hanging in the air. What could Vijay have done?'

'I don't know, Nish...I really don't. He could have walked up to the cops and told them the story. You guys caught up with Noor, eventually, didn't you?'

'But the pictures and the video would have been all over the place. How...'

'Do you think for a moment, Nish, that the son-of-a-bitch would have simply handed the pictures back to...to him... after the series? Would he be stupid enough to kill the goose?'

'No, he wouldn't,' she admitted.

'So it was all a bloody waste! He could have at least been man enough to own up to his...his faults...and at least not jackknifed his own team. Man, how could you do that? To your own brothers!'

'Nick...'

'And you, Nish...or perhaps I should say Inspector Nisha Chinappa of the Karnataka State Police. Do I really know you? The fresh-out-of-college girl that I fell for, the journalist who took me to the Chinnaswamy Stadium that fateful day, or this new avatar...speaking of the journalist...was that really an accident? Or did you have it planned all along?'

'Nick, I...had to have a way to get into the team...'

I couldn't believe what I was hearing. 'So you planted me!'

'I had no choice, Nick...The cops needed me to get closer to the team so that I could smoke out the rat. So, Gaurav and I worked on this plan to pick...pick a novice and hook him up with the team...so that...so that I could have a valid reason to be around the team hotel. We wanted an insider, Nick.'

'So that incident at Koshy's? That altercation with Gaurav?'

'All false. We did that just to find a reason for me to start talking to you.'

'Why me, Nish?' I could barely keep the anguish out of my voice.

'We had been observing you for a while, Nick. Quite unknown to you, Gaurav here had been shadowing teams in Bangalore for a month before we zeroed in on...on your friend, Sainath.'

'Bonsai!' I reeled under the impact of this revelation. 'You mean I was not even your first choice?'

Nisha kept her eyes on the floor. I could barely discern a slight shake of her head.

'Then...how...how come, I....' my voice trailed off.

Nisha looked up. 'We thought it would be easier to plant

a wicketkeeper-batsman in the team rather than a pace bowler. That evening we waited for you guys to show up at Koshy's, as Gaurav's research had shown you would. But then something unexpected happened. Instead of Bonsai ogling at me, as we had expected, you did. Still, Gaurav had all the intention of roughing up Bonsai when he walked up to your table. But even as he got there, Bonsai disappeared to the washroom and Gaurav had to improvise. We just couldn't afford to waste any more time.'

'And that stint at the Chinnaswamy? The spell that supposedly earned me a place in the team? Was that for real?'

'Nick, can't we just let that be?' she pleaded.

'I can't, Nish...I need to know. Was that for real?'

I dreaded her answer. When it came, it was like a sledgehammer to the solar plexus.

'The cops fixed it up, Nick...I spoke to Bill Cramer and explained that we suspected a possibility of match-fixing in the Pakistan series. We hooked him on to the plan and the man agreed to play along. He had no option, really...'

'So all those stats he reeled out to the media? All those wonderful comments on my ability and all that delightful sounding crap?'

'That was true, Nick. We didn't expect you to do so well in that session at the nets. It just made it all look credible...It made it easier to get you in the team so that I could wheedle my way in.'

I held on to a chair for support and steadied myself.

'Cramer had no intention of playing you initially, Nick... but when he saw what you were capable of...'

She didn't get beyond that, because at that moment the door swung open and Bill stuck his head in.

'Hey…you boys ready? My god, what happened to you? You look like you've been out drinking all night…Have you?'

'No, Bill…we are fine,' I said. 'Only Vijay won't be playing today.'

'Oh! So the news leaked out, did it?'

To say that we were shocked would have been a gross understatement. We were shell-shocked! For a moment, we thought that Vijay's secret was out in the open. I think a faint moan escaped Vijay's lips.

'Vijay, I had wanted to talk to you in private about this… but since you guys already seem to know, well, yes, it's true. We want you to sit out this game…sorry, buddy…take it easy, man.'

That last statement, I thought, was quite unnecessary. There was nothing but relief writ large on Vijay's face.

Bill's eyes fell on Nisha. 'Hey, what are you doing here, Nisha?'

I put an arm around Bill's shoulders and escorted him out. 'C'mon Bill, we've got a match to win.'

32

Final Rites at Bangalore

$\mathcal{W}$e didn't beat Pakistan in the final game. We demolished them. We gave them a beating that seven generations of Pakistani cricketers would remember and quail at.

Yaj was in a particularly murderous mood and looked happier than he had been in a long time. His newfound bliss, we'd later realize, was the outcome of an emotional reunion with his estranged girlfriend…the mysterious person he had rushed off to meet at the Golden Sand. And the 'one mistake' that he had been so piped about was now biding his time inside her womb, hopefully secure in the knowledge that his parents were happily together again.

In this highly exalted state of mind, Yaj descended upon the hapless Pakistanis like a storm of biblical proportions, and belted them to all corners of the park, sending them on a massive leather-hunt.

I carried some of my own good form from the previous game and made the most of an unexpected promotion up the order at number eight to score forty-six runs in less than no time. As a commentator described it, my knock was a 'throwing-the-kitchen-sink-at-it' effort. But I didn't care. My body was pumping a steady stream of adrenalin into my blood and I was going hell-for-leather. I was so pumped up that when I eventually holed out in the deep, I had to be almost carried off the field.

The newspaper that had adopted me as their darling blue-eyed baby carried an endearing picture of Yaj gently persuading me to move away from the pitch, as I stood my ground looking like a storm cloud.

We set them a mammoth 336 to get, with Yaj scoring a blazing hundred.

Then, even before Pakistanis had recovered from the bludgeoning they had just received, Roshan and Shiv ripped the heart out of their resistance, leaving them tottering at 36 for 6, off twelve overs. Guru and I delivered the final rites as we polished the tail off within the thirtieth over. The famed Pakistani batting lineup had been sent packing for a mere 95 runs.

It was a resounding victory. We had won the Friendship Cup 3-2. Yaj was deservedly the man of the match. I was slightly taken aback when I was picked as the man of the series. I remember walking to the podium in a daze, induced by the draining of the adrenalin from my system, and saying a few blade words about how glad I was for all the support from my team and the spectators.

As I went around the Chinnaswamy on the bike I won, to the accompaniment of thunderous applause, I felt strangely empty. As if all the happiness that I had earned and should have felt had been drained out.

33

Stumps

$\mathscr{A}$ day after our historic win, a press conference was called. There, in front of a gaggle of disbelieving media personnel, surrounded by a few glum-looking officials of the Cricket Board, Vijay Sehgal brought the curtains down on an illustrious career.

I watched the coverage of this conference at home. His speech was emotional, but strangely, he seemed at peace. He did not seem to have a care in the world.

Earlier, immediately after the game and the presentation ceremony, Vijay had addressed the team. In fact, he had poured his heart out, saying all...holding back nothing. He did not beg for forgiveness. He didn't need to, because his confession said it all.

As expected, a stony silence descended upon the room. Then, Monty rose and faced the team. 'We have all heard what Vijay had to say,' he began. 'I refuse to either condone or condemn him or his actions. How you want to react to this,' he said, looking once around the room, 'I leave to your discretion.' Saying so, he walked up to Vijay, patted him on the shoulders and walked out. One-by-one, all of us filed out of the room. As I walked out, I knew that these fine men would find forgiveness in their hearts, but it would take some time in coming.

I had not met or spoken to Nisha since I walked out of the hotel room the day before. As I sat there watching the emotional press conference unfold, I felt this keen desire to meet her. I picked up my phone from the table and dialed her number.

Five minutes later, I was on my way to the Chinnaswamy. The curtains had also come down on another glittering career. After nearly three decades of service to the Hariharan household, the faithful Lambretta had decided to hang up its carburetors. Its place was now taken by the brand new CBR 250R I had won the other day.

I didn't need an ID to get through, this time. The burly guard waved me through with a smart salute, stopping me only long enough for me to sign an autograph for his son.

I walked towards the North Stand and sat behind the sightscreen. There was some local game going on attended by a smattering of spectators dispersed all over the other stands in the stadium.

I had not done too badly, I admitted to myself. When everyone had sobered down enough after the party on that historic day, Bill and Monty had proudly announced how I was an integral part of their plans for the tour of South Africa the following month.

I couldn't help thinking that had the Karnataka police's strategy worked to plan, Bonsai would have been in the team instead of me. He may or may not have helped solve the case. His life may or may not have been in danger. He may or may not have won the man of the series. He may or may not have fallen in love with Nisha.

It was the last thought that hurt the most.

'Hi!'

She was standing next to me with a may-I-sit-down-beside-you look.

'Hi,' I responded. She sat down. For some time, an awkward silence continued to hang about like a guest who had walked into the wrong party.

'Aren't you going to say something, Nick?'

'What's there to say?'

'Well, I'm sure there's something to say. You were the one who called me here, remember?'

She was right. There was no way I could play the silent, suffering martyr after having called her here. I could have bloody well done that at home.

'What happens to Vijay, now?' I asked.

'What happens to him?'

I was beginning to get irritated. 'I mean the man has suffered enough. And it is not like he was some kind of serial offender. So, what are you gonna do with the evidence?'

'I should do the right thing, shouldn't I?'

'So you are gonna take action against the man? Have a

heart, Nish...the man did what he did because he was mortally scared...he was fighting to save his reputation, his family... moreover, he was fighting his conscience, too...I wonder how that man slept at night...perhaps he didn't...and now are we going to nail him...just because it is your duty?'

'I never said anything about duty, Nick...I just said that I should do the right thing.' Saying so, she pulled out the thick envelope and handed it to me.

I took the envelope. 'What about the shootout? How do you explain the deaths of Noor and his men?'

'Noor was a wanted man. Gaurav planted the gun he used to shoot those men in Noor's hands before we escaped from the cabin. He has arranged for the whole episode to look like a tiff between the three men that ended with Noor shooting the two others. A post mortem report would perhaps report the anomaly of finding a bullet from the gun that Noor supposedly handled, in his own body. But I don't think there would be much of an investigation. Even if there were, it would be inconclusive. Gaurav wiped the place clean of any telltale finger prints that you or Vijay would have left behind.'

'Why are you doing all this? Don't you want to take in the glory for having busted a match-fixing racket?'

'So you are not buying the idea that I might actually be feeling for Vijay? You want to believe that I might have some ulterior motive?' She took a deep breath and turned her face away from me to stare into the distance for a while. When she turned to face me again, her face was resolute.

'Nick, you are right. I do have an ulterior motive. The evidence I have collected during the investigation will not hold.

What I have is a set of photographs, which will only show up one of India's greatest cricketers as a sorry ass of a pervert. It will not even remotely link him with match-fixing. Nick, I am a cop, not a sting-operation journalist. Then what I have is a recording, which sounds like Vijay talking to someone about some boy, his girlfriend and with the word 'kidnap' thrown in. What does that prove? Nothing! I also didn't record Vijay's confession, Nick. The only guy who could have thrown some light on the whole episode, Noor, is dead. So, you see, what I have is a case that cannot be proved in court. Does that answer your question?'

'What if Noor had more copies of the evidence stocked up somewhere? What if some accomplice of his could still go ahead and do the dirty work?'

'Unlikely. The man operated alone. Don't you find it strange that he chose to contact Vijay all on his own, rather than send an accomplice, and mastermind the entire operation from the shadows? Point is that the man trusted no one. I seriously doubt he has any other copies of the photographs or the CDs anywhere else. If I am wrong and there are other copies around, we won't be able to do much about it. It would come out sooner or later and Vijay would have to bear the consequences.'

'Hmmm…'

'Nick, do you believe in God?'

'Yes, why do you ask?'

'Because I think God will not let that happen. Like you said, Vijay has suffered enough. I don't think God will put him through another trial. I think this case is closed.'

'Not quite. There is one more thing to settle.'

She looked surprised. 'There is? What?'

'What happens to us?'

The startled look remained in her eyes for a second and then slowly the smile that had been missing through the conversation returned to her eyes.

'I thought you'd never ask. What about us, Nick?'

'Well, I think I might be on that tour of South Africa next month…and your assignments are gonna keep you busy for a bit, I think…so, don't we need to work out the details of how to manage a long distance relationship?'

'Now we are talking!'

'That's the problem…we are talking when we should rather be doing something else.'

'Oooo,' she said, rolling her eyes and drawing closer. 'And what would that be, Nikhil Hariharan?'

'Are you a good kisser?'

'Why don't you find out?'

It was a beautiful moon that rose over the Chinnaswamy that night.

Acknowledgements

To the Supreme Being, whose reassuring and benevolent presence I have always felt.

To Mom and Dad, who shared my frustrations and joys, as I trudged along on this maiden voyage.

To Divya, for bringing a sense of balance and purpose to my life.

To Meenakshi Singh at Rupa, for her kind, helpful and immensely patient guidance always.

To Jai, soldier, poet, philosopher, dearest of brothers and the man I have looked up to always.

To Renu and Geethu, my pillars of strength and lights in the darkest of places when all other lights went out.

To Vimal, my brother, for being my best friend and for just being himself.

To all my friends, colleagues and well-wishers, who have contributed in many ways to this work.

And to Baba, most of all, for introducing me to books, unshackling my imagination and showing me a world far richer and beautiful than the one we inhabit. Are you the ONE whose presence and benevolence I always feel?